HAPPY EVER AFTER AT THE COTSWOLDS CANDY STORE

HANNAH LYNN

Boldwood

First published in Great Britain in 2025 by Boldwood Books Ltd.

A CIP catalogue record for this book is available from the British Library.

Paperback ISBN 978-1-83656-007-4

Hardback ISBN 978-1-83656-006-7

Ebook ISBN 978-1-83656-008-1

Kindle ISBN 978-1-83656-009-8

This book is printed on certified sustainable paper. Boldwood Books is dedicated to putting sustainability at the heart of our business. For more information please visit https://www.boldwoodbooks.com/about-us/sustainability/

Boldwood Books Ltd, 23 Bowerdean Street, London, SW6 3TN

www.boldwoodbooks.com

ALSO BY HANNAH LYNN

The Cotswolds Candy Store Series

Second Chances at the Cotswold Candy Store

Love Blooms at the Cotswold Candy Store

Family Ties at the Cotswolds Candy Store

High Hopes at the Cotswolds Candy Store

Sunny Days at the Cotswolds Candy Store

A Summer Wedding at the Cotswolds Candy Store

Snowflakes Over the Cotswolds Candy Store

Happy Ever After at the Cotswolds Candy Store

The Wildflower Lock Series

New Beginnings at Wildflower Lock

Coffee and Cake at Wildflower Lock

Blue Skies Over Wildflower Lock

Forever Love at Wildflower Lock

Standalone Novels

In at the Deep End

The Side Hustle

Hannah Lynn writing as H.M Lynn

The Head Teacher

The Student

The Valentine's Date

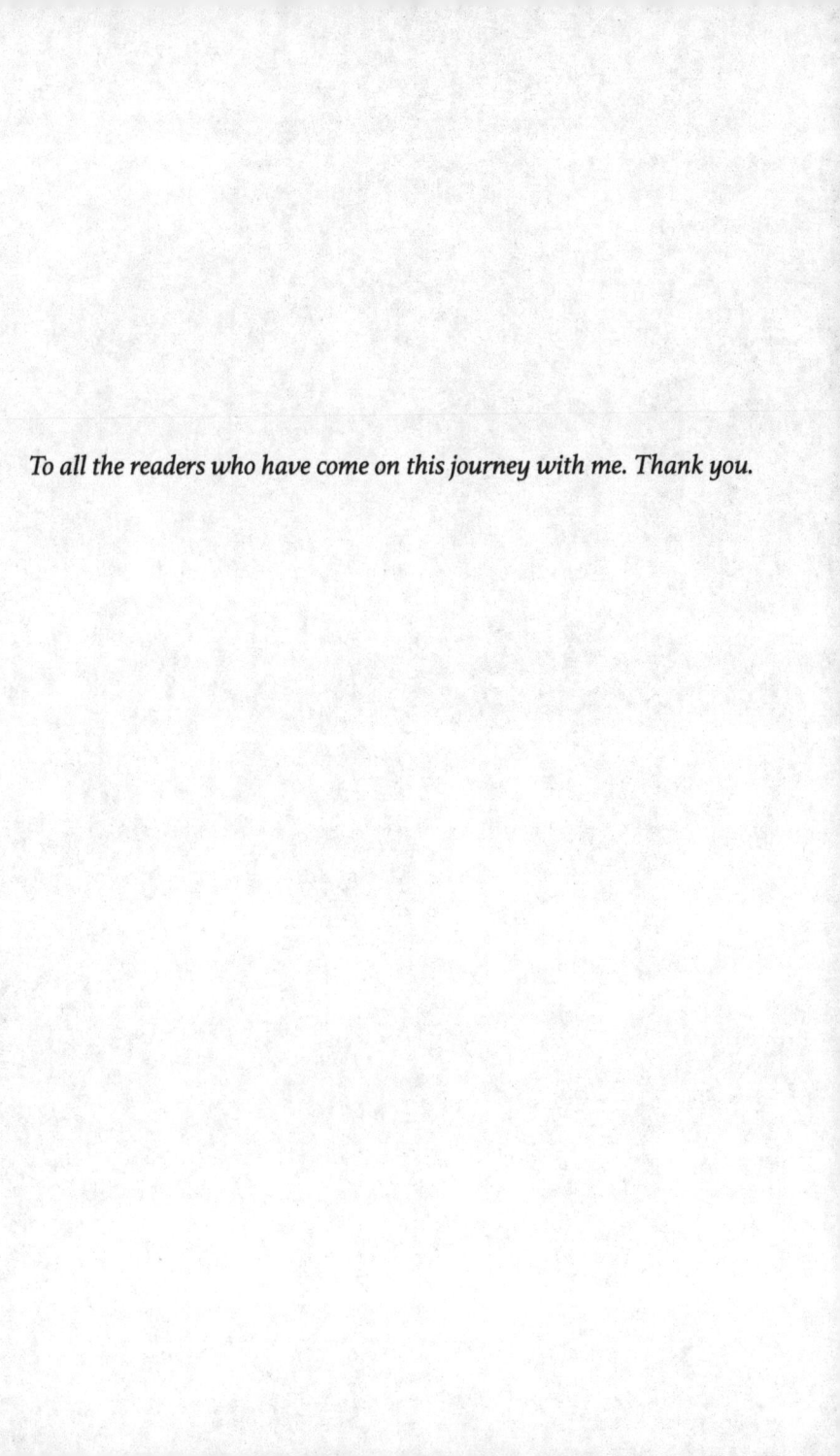

To all the readers who have come on this journey with me. Thank you.

1

A sweet citrus scent filled the air as Holly weighed out the sherbet lemons.

'That will be one pound twenty, please,' she said as she handed the bag to the customer. Not that she needed to say the price. Mrs Heggings had the same order of sherbet lemons every time she came in. Which was always on a Thursday, always before midday and always after a cup of coffee at the tearoom on the green. She was so regular that Holly could have pre-packed her sweets ready for her visit, the same way she could for so many of her customers who made visiting Just One More part of their weekly routine, but she didn't want to be presumptuous. Besides, she liked the conversations they had while she was fetching the jars and filling the bags. They made her feel like she was part of the community. Which she definitely was. Ten years of running a sweet shop in the centre of a village like Bourton-on-the-Water would do that for you.

'I hope this weather makes up its mind soon,' Mrs Heggings said as she handed Holly the money. 'You know, I left this morning with a thick jumper and a coat on, and look at it now.

It's stunning. Like summer came two months early. But they say it's going to be showers this afternoon. Even with a sky as clear as that one out there.'

Weather was always a hot topic of conversation in the sweet shop, and often a source of complaint for many regulars, but Holly would listen and nod along like she agreed, because she knew that sometimes, it wasn't about the weather at all. It was about the customers feeling like someone was listening to them. Which was what she always tried to do. Provided the queue behind them wasn't too long.

'I'll take all the sunny days I can get,' Holly said. 'But I don't mind the odd shower now and then. It drives the customers in.'

Mrs Heggings laughed. 'Well, I better get a move on,' she said, dropping her sweets into her wicker basket. 'I don't want it to start raining before I get home. Have a lovely weekend.'

'You too,' Holly said.

As Mrs Heggings headed to the door, the next customer stepped forward.

'Can I get a quarter of pear drops and a half of butter-scotch?' he asked. Mr Peterson was another regular, although one who liked to vary his choice in boiled sweets now and then.

'Absolutely,' Holly said. 'Let me just grab those for you.'

As Holly moved across the shop, he carried on talking.

'So, any exciting plans this weekend? Are you doing anything nice with that wonderful daughter of yours?'

'Well, I'm in the shop tomorrow,' Holly replied. 'She's with her dad, but we've got a lovely family day planned on Sunday with our friends.'

'Sounds wonderful. You know, it won't be long until she's old enough to help you here.'

'No,' Holly agreed as she placed the jars of sweets on the

counter ready to weigh out, 'it won't. I can't believe how quickly the time has gone.'

She'd often used that expression in the past, particularly when talking about busy summers in the shop or holidays that felt as though they had whizzed past, but it wasn't until she'd had Hope that she realised how true it was. Time moved so quickly now. Somehow, her daughter had just turned seven years old. Seven. It felt like only yesterday she had been a tiny baby. Or a toddler flushing her toy rabbits down the toilet. Of course, it would be a long time before she could actually work in the shop with Holly, but she liked nothing more than coming in after school and helping straighten up the shelves and, obviously, testing a fair bit of the produce too.

As Holly weighed out the pear drops, her eyes fell on the diamond ring that sparkled on her finger. Over half a decade had passed since Evan had died, but she still wore the ring on her finger. In some ways, it felt like that was the only thing which had stayed the same. Her life had changed so much since then.

Hope had started school; that was a big adjustment, particularly for Holly's mother, who had spent so much time looking after her while Holly worked. Her father had retired. Holly had employed two new members of staff and, on the more personal side of things, had sold the house that she and Evan had renovated together. Even though she knew selling up and downsizing made sense, she had gone back and forth for over a year after his death, trying to work out the right thing to do. The house held so many memories for her, and selling it felt like she was letting all of those go. But it was a strange twist of fate that suddenly made the decision that much easier.

Ben, Hope's dad, had wanted to buy a place with his girl-friend, Georgia, which meant selling his three-bed house that was right next door to Jamie's place. At that point, Jamie had three children under three – the twins having been a very exciting surprise – and she and Holly had been leaning on one another for support more than ever. It all felt so serendipitous that she thought Ben was just selling up for her sake, but after several serious conversations about work and so on, she knew that wasn't the case. Now she had been living there for almost four years, and she couldn't be happier.

As she took Mr Peterson's payment, Holly readied herself to serve the next person in the queue when a voice rang out from the back of the shop.

'I'm so sorry I'm late, Holly. There are blooming roadworks. I knew I shouldn't've taken the car. I should've just walked, but I thought it would be easier to pick the kids up later, given all the blooming clubs they need driving to. But of course, I couldn't find a car parking space.'

Caroline was slipping on her blue and white striped apron as she spoke, hurrying her way through the customers around Holly to the till.

'I'll take over,' she said. 'You haven't had a break yet.'

It was true – Holly had been in the shop since nine o'clock, and it was now two thirty, but somehow she didn't seem to mind that much. Some days, talking to customers like Mr Peterson and other regulars just felt like a day chatting with friends. But as her stomach growled, she knew she probably had to get something to eat.

'That would be great, if you're sure?'

'No problem at all,' Caroline said before shifting her attention from Holly to the customer. 'Ever so sorry about that. What can I get you?'

As Caroline carried on serving, Holly headed up the stairs. She had just reached the small stockroom, packed floor to ceiling with bags and boxes of sweets, when her phone rang. Giles's name flashed up on the screen.

There was no need for a surname. Giles Caverty, who was once a nemesis and now one of her very best friends, was the only Giles in her life. It was rare that she would go a week without seeing him, and she normally spoke to him most days too, but that tended to be in the evening rather than the middle of the day, when he knew she was likely working. Still, she picked up the phone and answered the call.

'Hey, what's up?'

'Are you busy right now? Is Caroline in the shop?' Giles was normally the epitome of politeness, and offered at least some form of greeting when she answered, but the double questions without even a quick 'how are you doing', immediately put Holly on edge.

'I'm just on my lunch break. Why? Is something wrong?'

'Not exactly.'

'Not exactly? What does that mean?'

A slight pause filled the air before he spoke again.

'I may have had a little bit of an accident,' he said.

2

'Are you okay to lock up?' Holly said to Caroline as she raced down the stairs. Her heart pounded as she slung her handbag over her shoulder and took the bottom step so fast, she nearly slipped into the shelves. Thankfully, she righted herself in time.

'Is everything okay?' Caroline asked.

Holly made a movement somewhere between a shrug and a shake of her head.

'I'm not sure. It's Giles; he's at the hospital.'

'What? Why?'

'I don't know. He just asked me to pick him up. He didn't say what happened. I'll ring you when I have some idea.'

Caroline nodded. 'Okay, go, go. I've got things covered here.' Holly carried on towards the door, though she had only put one foot outside when Caroline called again. 'Don't forget, you've still got your apron on.'

Holly looked down and, true enough, she was still wearing her blue and white uniform. She didn't stop to take it off, though. What did her clothes matter? She needed to get to the hospital now.

Sweat dampened Holly's hands as she gripped the steering wheel.

'He's fine. He's going to be fine.' She kept her breaths deep as she spoke aloud, hoping that either the speaking or the breathing would help slow the panic that was coursing through her. But as she drove out of the village and towards the town, it was near impossible to stop her thoughts from running wild. 'He's going to be fine. He rang me. He asked me to pick him up. If it had been that serious, the doctors wouldn't have let him ring, would they? They would've had somebody else call me, wouldn't they?'

They were rhetorical questions, which she was almost certain she knew the answers to, but it still didn't help the anxiety that was building more and more with every mile she drove.

Maybe it was nothing to do with Giles at all, she considered. Maybe it was Faye, his sister, who'd had the accident.

She was the one who worked at the hospital, after all. Maybe something happened to her, and Giles wanted Holly there beside him. But then, why wouldn't he say that? And Faye had a husband now. No, it wouldn't be to do with Faye, but now she couldn't remember exactly how Giles had worded himself. Had he said *there's been an accident*, or *I've had an accident*? Why couldn't she remember?

As Holly drove into the hospital car park, an ambulance siren rang out loudly in front of her. Her throat tightened and her pulse kicked up another notch. For a long time after Evan's death, the sound of a siren would have caused her to shut down entirely. It happened once in the sweet shop. She hadn't been long back at work when an ambulance had rushed down the High Street. Holly had frozen, her hand shaking, the bag of sweets rattling in her grasp as images of the day she had lost Evan rose to the surface of her mind.

Her father had been there at that moment and, seeing what

was happening, took control of the situation. He got her to sit down at the bottom of the stairs while he dealt with the customer, then switched the sign on the door to *Closed*. For nearly an hour, he had sat there beside her, holding her hand, waiting for the moment to pass. And it had, eventually. Since then, there had been several ambulances down the High Street and though they always caused her heart rate to rise a little, that was it. The images of Evan would float into her mind, then drift away again.

But what if she lost Giles, too?

Since the accident, she had done everything in her power to mitigate anything happening to her friends, including taking every first-aid course available to her. She had taken an adult first-aid course, a paediatric first-aid course and first-aid training for sailing and water sports, which involved hefty travelling to the nearest sailing club, but felt necessary after what she had been through with Evan. She had even considered training to become a volunteer first responder too, but hadn't yet got around to it. Still, all the training in the world didn't mean anything if she wasn't there to help the people she loved in the moments they needed her.

Her heart was in her mouth as she rushed through the double doors of the hospital towards the reception.

'I'm here to see Giles Caverty,' she said, tears thickening in her throat. 'He was in an accident. I don't know what sort. He just rang me and said I needed to come.'

'Yes, just one second,' the nurse said as she tapped away at the screen. 'Caverty?'

'Yes.'

'Great. He's on Ward 3. Take the elevator to the third floor, then turn right. You'll see the signs for it.'

Holly didn't even thank the nurse as she turned and raced towards the elevator.

The tears that had filled her throat were now glazing her eyes. She couldn't do it. She couldn't lose someone else.

3

Holly followed the signs to Ward 3 and, after a couple of turns, including one wrong one, found herself standing in front of a set of double doors. Her hands were trembling as she pushed it open and stepped forward, yet before she could even ask the nurse what room Giles was in, a familiar-sounding voice called her name.

'Holly?'

Holly spun around.

'Faye!'

With a near gasp flying from her lips, Holly wrapped her arms around Giles's sister, before quickly breaking away again. 'Where is he? What happened? Is he okay? Can I see him?'

'He's just through there,' Faye said, pointing to a curtained-off area. 'And he's fine, just his ego's a bit bruised. Well, his ego and lots of other places, really. But it's nothing serious. He'll be glad to see you. I'll give you a moment.'

With tears running down her cheeks, Holly stepped through the curtain. Her heart leapt. Giles was sitting upright in bed. A line of several stitches crossed from the inside of his eyebrow up towards his hairline, while a thick, white plaster had been placed across his obviously broken nose. There were bruises beneath his eyes and across his arms too, yet despite having to be in an excessive amount of pain, the moment he saw her, he was on his feet.

'Oh my God. You scared the life out of me.' She fell into his chest, only for him to wince audibly. Hurriedly, she stepped away. 'I'm sorry—'

'No, no, I'm so sorry,' Giles said, shaking his head. 'I was an idiot. I didn't think. I shouldn't have called you. It was when I hung up that I realised you'd probably start panicking and thinking the worst and I should've—'

'Don't be silly. I'm glad you called me,' Holly said. 'Of course you call me. You know that.'

Giles grimaced. 'I tried to ring you back. To tell you it wasn't anything serious, but you didn't pick up.'

'I didn't hear it ring,' Holly said, before realising the reason. 'I left my phone in the shop. I just dumped it and ran. And it looks serious. That's a lot of stitches.'

'Fourteen,' he answered, before adding a slanted smirk. 'But I told them to make it look impressive. You know how the ladies love scars.'

She couldn't help but laugh, even if it was a stupid comment. The relief she felt was palpable.

'What did you do?' Holly asked. 'Don't tell me you crashed a car?'

This time, Giles's grimace was purely one of humour. 'Come on, you know I'd never do this in the car. I'm a wonderful driver. No, I was out on my uncle's quad bike. I'd lost a couple of sheep, and I thought that would be the quickest way to find them. I haven't actually been on a quad bike since I was about sixteen.

Turns out, I'm not quite as good at handling the bumps as I used to be.'

'You were on a quad bike?' Holly repeated.

'Yeah, I know. I remember them being a lot more fun than— Ow!' Giles winced as Holly punched him on the shoulder.

'Don't you dare do that again,' she said, then punched him once more. 'You nearly gave me a heart attack. Do you know what could've happened to you? You're lucky you only ended up with stitches.'

'I know, I know. I'm sorry. Like I said, I shouldn't have rung you.'

'What? You think it would have been better if you'd kept this hidden from me? Trust me, you'd have been in even more trouble. You know you're Hope's favourite uncle?'

The look of pain that had been etched on Giles' face transformed into a small smirk.

'I know I am,' he said. 'She told you that, right? I definitely am. And I'm your favourite too, right? Out of all your friends, I'm definitely the best.'

Holly's heart was still pounding, but for some reason, her throat had also gone inexplicably dry. Giles was one of the most important people in the world to her; there was no way around that. These past few years, he had been there for her every step of the way, and she simply couldn't imagine life without him.

'You know what you mean to me,' she said. Her words came out quieter than anticipated and his eyes locked on hers. Once again, she felt her pulse rising. Giles shifted slightly, moving his hand as if he was going to reach out and touch her. She drew in a long breath, wondering if she wanted him to do that and, at the same time, wondering why it mattered if he did. They often held hands. Why would this be anything different? With her heart drumming behind her ears, she held her breath, waiting.

Then the curtain swept back.

'Giles, sweetie, why didn't you call me? It's all right now, darling. Your baby girl is here. Your sweetie pie is here. I'm here for you, honeybun.'

4

Holly stepped back from the bed and tried not to roll her eyes. There, standing in the cubicle with them, was a perfectly manicured, pristinely dressed young woman who looked like she belonged on the front of some country life magazine, rather than the harshly lit, antiseptic-smelling hospital ward. As always, everything about her was perfect, from the application of her makeup to her choice of accessories to her straight, white teeth. She was the type of woman you found plenty of in the Cotswolds, normally driving around in a Land Rover, probably with a picnic basket filled with champagne and pâté in the back as she and her friends headed for a weekend at the races.

'Sienna?' Giles said, his voice laced with shock. 'I didn't expect to see you. What are you doing here?'

'What do you mean? Of course I came. You had an accident. Why else would I be here?'

'Of course, I... I realise that,' Giles stuttered. 'What I mean is, well – who told you?'

With an exasperated sigh, Sienna swept past Holly and dropped her handbag down on the chair.

'I went to the manor. Business. One of the charities is interested in partnering with your uncle, but anyway, when I got there, the groundsman told me what had happened. Obviously, I came straight here. And it's a good job I did. You're an absolute mess. You obviously need me.'

'Honestly, it's just a few stitches.'

'It's a head injury, Giles. Clearly, you're going to need constant supervision for the next twenty-four hours in case there's a concussion. Honestly, I'm amazed. What would have happened if I hadn't turned up?'

Holly cleared her throat. It was possible that Sienna was just so upset and worried that she hadn't even noticed Holly was there. After all, shock did different things to different people. And so she stepped forward.

'It's fine, Sienna. He rang me. I was going to drive him home whenever he was ready. After he's been discharged, that is.'

For the first time since she'd stepped into the room, Sienna's eyes flickered to Holly. The action was minuscule, as was the purse of her lips, but the sigh she emitted afterwards was impressively long.

'Darling,' she said, her attention once again focused on Giles. 'Everything's fine. I'm here now, it's fine. I'll be the one to look after you. After all, that's what a good girlfriend does.'

Holly could feel her teeth grinding together. She and Sienna were from different worlds. She got that. But that didn't mean Sienna had to act like she didn't exist. She was about to say something along those lines when the curtain was swept aside for a second time and Faye stepped inside.

'Wow, look at this.' Faye's bright smile was a welcome respite from Sienna's surliness. 'It's quite an entourage of women you've got here. If I didn't know any better, I'd say you did all this for the attention.' She looked at Holly with a grin that Holly reciprocated. But on the other side of the room, Sienna looked as if she'd just been slapped across the face. Her eyes widened and her jaw locked as she took a step towards Faye.

'How dare you?' she hissed, her voice a low quiver. 'I am absolutely appalled by your audacity. Can't you see how much pain he's in? I want the name of your supervisor this instant. That type of behaviour is totally unprofessional and unacceptable.'

Holly step forwards.

'Sienna, it's—'

'I don't care if she meant it as a joke or otherwise. I'm absolutely disgusted.'

'Sienna, this is—'

'No, don't make excuses for her. It's outright unprofessional. A sackable offence, if you ask me.'

Sienna wasn't listening, and Faye was so stunned, her jaw was hanging wide open, speechless. In the confusion, Holly and Giles exchanged a look, followed by a short nod.

'Sienna!' they yelled simultaneously. The noise was enough to cause a glass of water on the table to ripple, but it also had the desired effect of stunning Sienna into silence, at which point, Giles finally managed to get a word in edgeways.

'Sienna, this is my sister, Faye.'

'Your sister?' A second later, the penny dropped and Sienna's cheeks coloured as vibrantly as her hot-pink lipstick.

'Oh my goodness, I'm so sorry. I didn't realise. I thought you worked with babies.'

'I do,' Faye said. 'But obviously, when you hear your big brother's been in an accident, you're allowed to come check on him.'

'Yes, yes, of course.' Sienna's voice was so breathy with panic, Holly almost felt sorry for her. 'Of course, I realise that now. Yes, and obviously, I'm not going to make any complaints. I was just a little highly strung with worry, you understand? It's ever so lovely to meet you,' she added, before grabbing her hand and kissing her enthusiastically on both cheeks. 'I've heard so much about you. It's such a joy to finally put a face to the name. We need to meet up properly, outside here. Cocktails, perhaps? Giles makes an incredible old-fashioned, but you probably already know that.' She let out a tight, high-pitched laugh.

Holly watched on as Faye waited to be released. While she couldn't remember exactly when she had first met Sienna, she was sure Giles's current girlfriend hadn't been nearly this enthusiastic.

'That would be nice,' Faye said, stepping back the moment Sienna let go of her. 'And talking of catching up, Holly, we are due a coffee soon too. It's been forever.'

'I know. I haven't seen you since the boys' first birthday party.'

'Which is almost a year ago. Crazy, right? It seems like forever since I've seen Hope too. She must be so big now.'

'She's seven. Would you believe it?'

Faye let out a groan. 'You know, it seems like only last week when you arrived at the hospital, and I was forced to lie and say all your friends were actually relatives.'

The pair giggled. Holly owed Faye. She was the reason that Hope was delivered, surrounded by love and friendship, and if she hadn't lied, Holly would have been forced to bring her daughter into the world without them.

'You know you're welcome at mine whenever you want,' Holly said. 'And there's plenty of room to bring the boys. Especially when the weather's nice. Jamie and I have finally taken the plunge to remove the fence between the gardens. Oh, and we got a kitten.'

'You did?'

'Rhubarb. Hope named her. You'll have to bring your two over to meet her.'

'Oh, they would love that.'

'Any time you want. Just give me a call.'

Holly was about to turn the conversation around to Faye; ask how her daughters and husband were doing, and if she got the promotion she'd gone for at work recently, but before she could get another word out, Sienna coughed loudly.

For a split second, Holly felt a little guilty. She hadn't meant to ostracise Sienna from the conversation, but something about her stony face told her that was exactly how Sienna felt. Ostracised and angered. Holly opened her mouth, ready to apologise, but before she could, Sienna sniffed, then angled her chin ever so slightly so she was looking down her nose towards Holly.

'Well, as lovely as this reunion is, I think it's time I got my boyfriend home. Thank you, Holly, but I don't think we need you any more.'

5

'I'm not sure I ever disliked one of Giles's girlfriends as much as I dislike Sienna,' Holly said to Jamie. They were sitting in the garden. Just as Holly had explained to Faye only a couple of hours beforehand, she and Jamie had removed the fence between the two semi-detached houses, creating one enormous backyard. It wasn't something they had considered when Holly and Hope moved in and the first year there, it had been fine keeping it as two separate spaces, but the next year, Hope and Jamie's eldest, Randall, had spent so much time climbing over the thin wooden frame, Holly was sure there was going to be an accident and decided to put a gate in. Then, when the twins were old enough to walk, the gate swinging non-stop back and forth, they gave in and removed the fence entirely.

'You should've heard the way she spoke to me.' Holly took a sip of her wine. Rhubarb, the kitten, was busy pouncing on a dandelion just a few feet away. 'The way she just dismissed me. And after Giles had rung me to pick him up.'

'I've had a couple of interesting conversations with her,' Fin said, topping up his own glass of homemade kombucha. 'We were talking the other day about her work in the charity sector. You know she puts a lot of hours into that job. And it's always for great causes.'

'It's probably easy to put a lot of hours into a job when you're getting paid six figures,' Holly said. 'No, she is absolutely not right for Giles, and the sooner he sees that, the better. Then again, they're about to hit the six-month mark, so I'm sure he'll be done with her soon.' She took a sip of her drink, feeling confident that at least Jamie would back her up, but instead, her friends exchanged a look.

'What? What is it?' she said. That wasn't just a casual glance. She could tell from the way Jamie's lips tightened.

'Don't tell me you like her? Is that it? Are you two secretly best buddies? God, please don't tell me you've asked her to be a guide-parent at the twins' naming day. Please don't tell me that.'

'No, it's not that.' Jamie laughed. She hadn't had any of her boys christened, but liked to have a naming ceremony for them when they were old enough to have some inclination of what was going on. This summer, when the twins turned three, they would have theirs, though as Holly was already a guide-parent to Randall, she didn't expect to be asked again.

'What is it?' she pressed. 'You don't actually think Sienna's a good match for him, do you?'

'Well...' Jamie looked at Fin again, whose mouth twisted up into a smirk, almost as if he was daring Jamie to say something delicate. But why would that be? What could Jamie possibly say that would upset Holly?

'The thing is, you've never actually liked any of Giles's girlfriends, have you?'

Holly thought about it. In the last three or four years, Giles had introduced them to numerous girlfriends, with the relationships ranging from anywhere between the three- or four-month mark to the far more serious nine- or ten-month mark. One, Joanna, had even broken the year, but not by much. Three weeks later and that relationship was over too.

'That's not true,' Holly said indignantly. 'I liked that one girl.'

'Which?'

'I can't remember her name. Rosie, I think it was.'

'The one who had already accepted a job abroad before they started dating and didn't want anything serious?'

'Yes, that's her.'

Jamie sighed as she shook her head, though Holly really couldn't understand why.

'Look, it's not my fault that he has a habit of picking women who are completely wrong for him. If he actually dated the right sort of person for once, then I'd like them. I know I would.'

'The right sort of person? So what would they be like?' Jamie asked.

Holly pondered the question for a moment. She'd never really considered what Giles's ideal partner should be like, only that it definitely hadn't been any of the women he'd dated so far.

'Someone mature to start with,' she said. 'Perhaps someone who is closer to thirty than twenty-one. Someone who is ready to settle down. That's what he needs.'

'Sienna fits that bill,' Fin said. 'She's twenty-seven, has a steady job... and while we're talking about jobs—'

'We weren't talking about jobs,' Jamie cut in. 'We were talking about Sienna.'

'Okay, fine, yes we were, but I want to talk about jobs now,' Fin said. 'I was talking to an old colleague of mine over in the States, about you, Holly.'

'You were?' If anyone else had mentioned a colleague, Holly could have bet the sweet shop that the conversation would continue on to the suggestion of a blind date. But Fin never did that. Maybe because of his closeness to Evan or maybe because he knew how Holly would respond.

'Yeah, he's opening up a chain of old-fashioned English sweet shops. They're all the rage at the minute in certain parts of the States. Apparently, he's been wanting to do it for a few years now, but they've finally found the first couple of locations they want to use. He wondered if you'd be interested in doing a bit of work for him?'

'A bit of work?' Holly asked, curious. 'Sorry, what does that mean? What kind of work?'

'Well, it depends on what you'd be available for. He asked if you'd be interested in going over there for six months, to help them set everything up. You know, make sure they've got a really authentic feel to their places. I said I didn't know if that would be possible, what with Hope and Ben and everything, so he suggested you could have a couple of short trips over there. Troubleshooting-type stuff.'

'Troubleshooting?' Holly repeated. 'I could have written an entire novel over the issues I had when I first took the place over from Maud, but I doubt he'll have any of those issues.'

'Well, he'd definitely like it if we could go out for a bit. Really help cement the whole traditional English thing.'

A job that involved travelling abroad? It had been something she'd dreamed of, but also thought was something reserved for people far more high-flying than her.

'I wonder if I could fit it in with a holiday,' Holly thought aloud.

'I can't see why not. Why don't I give you his number? He's a great guy, not going to mess you around or anything. And if you're not interested, just tell him that. What's the worst that can happen?'

What was the worst, indeed? The truth was, Holly had

thought about spreading her wings. She had seen several shops recently coming up for sale or lease in nearby villages – Moreton-in-Marsh, Cirencester, even the picturesque Lechlade had a little shop that had once been the post office, currently for sale. She couldn't help but daydream about making something there too. After all, she was sure she'd get a business loan, but did she want that work? It wasn't just a case of having a second location and having to work extra hours; it would mean finding more staff to run the place, dealing with more sicknesses, more holidays. This, however, wouldn't involve any of that. And it would mean getting to go to America.

'Sure,' she said. 'Why not? Pass on my number to him.'

A flutter of excitement filled her. It was good to have something positive to think of after the day she'd had.

Although Jamie was determined not to drop her issue.

'That all sounds incredible and everything, but we still haven't addressed the fact that you refuse to speak to Sienna.'

'I have spent time talking to her,' Holly said. 'Did you not listen to me at all? I spoke to her today, and I didn't like anything that I heard at all. No, we don't have anything in common.'

'That wasn't a proper conversation. You can't blame her for being a bit off. She was obviously stressed about Giles. Look, it's our anniversary party on Friday. You can sit next to her then, get to know her better that way.'

'That's this Friday?' Holly asked, her eyebrows leaping up with surprise. 'That's come around fast.'

'You're telling us,' Jamie said.

Fin and Jamie's wedding was the night when she and Evan had taken the plunge and decided to buy a house together. He had been so nervous. Worried about pushing their relationship too fast and ruining things. But she knew by then that when you were meant to be with one another, it didn't matter how fast or slow you took it. With a pang of nostalgia spreading through her, Holly looked out across the garden to where the children were currently arguing over who got the tyre swing. It could comfortably fit two people, but there were four children who always wanted it at the same time, which is why they had erected an identical one in Holly's half of the garden. Though, as they could have predicted, the children weren't anywhere near as interested in that one.

'I guess I need to sort out a babysitter, then,' Holly said, bringing herself back to the moment.

'It's all sorted. Tim and Izzy are going to do it,' Jamie said. 'Caroline sorted it with them weeks ago.'

'I still find it crazy that Tim and Izzy are old enough to babysit,' Holly said, though no matter how strange it felt for her, she suspected it was even odder for Caroline. Holly couldn't imagine Hope being almost old enough to fly the coop. Then again, a couple of years ago, she couldn't have imagined being mum to a seven-year-old. 'I guess it means we're really old too.'

'It does,' Jamie said. 'Which is how I know you'll be incredibly mature, sit next to Sienna and actually get to know her, like the rest of us have done. Because that's what being a friend means.'

'Fine, I'll get to know her,' Holly said. 'But if she's horrible to me again, then that's it. Friendship is off the cards for good. And you're not allowed to say nice things about her to me or try to change my mind, get it?'

'There's that maturity I was talking about.' Jamie smirked.

It was first thing the next morning when Holly rang Giles. She
had sent him a message the night before, just to check he got
home okay, and he had replied straight away to say everything
was fine and there was no need to worry, but you could say
anything in a text, couldn't you? She wanted to know how he
actually was. Whether he was in pain, or had been suffering with
dizziness or loss of sight. She wouldn't put it past him just to
pretend everything was all right to Sienna so that he didn't worry
her. But that wasn't Holly's only reason for calling him. Hope had
overheard her talking to Jamie and Fin about the accident and
had been so upset, she had needed to spend the night in Holly's
bed. Now Hope was up and desperate to speak to him, and Holly
knew she'd get no peace until she had.

'Will those stay in your head forever?' Hope said,
commenting on Giles's row of stitches.

'Nope. They'll disappear when my head's all healed,' Giles
replied.

'Disappear?'

'Yup. Like magic.'

6

It was first thing the next morning when Holly rang Giles. She
had sent him a message the night before, just to check he got
home okay, and he had replied straight away to say everything
was fine and there was no need to worry, but you could say
anything in a text, couldn't you? She wanted to know how he
actually was. Whether he was in pain, or had been suffering with
dizziness or loss of sight. She wouldn't put it past him just to
pretend everything was all right to Sienna so that he didn't worry
her. But that wasn't Holly's only reason for calling him. Hope had
overheard her talking to Jamie and Fin about the accident and
had been so upset, she had needed to spend the night in Holly's
bed. Now Hope was up and desperate to speak to him, and Holly
knew she'd get no peace until she had.

'Will those stay in your head forever?' Hope said,
commenting on Giles's row of stitches.

'Nope. They'll disappear when my head's all healed,' Giles
replied.

'Disappear?'

'Yup. Like magic.'

Hope turned to look at Holly excitedly. 'Can I get some? I want to see them disappearing. I'll record it on your phone. It'll be really cool.'

Holly raised her eyebrows at her daughter. 'No, you can't, and it won't be really cool to get stitches. Stitches mean you've hurt yourself. Hopefully, you won't ever need to have them. Now I thought you want to speak to Uncle Giles?'

With a slight pout on her lips, Hope turned back to look at the phone.

'Is it painful?' she said.

Giles shook his head. 'It should be. But it's not because the doctors have given Uncle Giles lots of nice tablets to make the pain go away.'

'Giles,' Holly snapped.

'What?' He let out a slight groan as he spoke again. 'Fine. The doctors have given Giles lots of nasty tablets to make the pain go away. Terribly bad things. I wish I didn't have to take them.'

He looked through the camera at Holly and smirked and, as much as she didn't want to, Holly couldn't help but reciprocate. He had a way of doing that, weakening her resolve and making her relent, although she could see what he'd said about the painkillers was true. There was a definite looseness to his expression that she hadn't seen before.

Hope opened her mouth with another question likely teetering on her tongue, when a loud voice squealed from offscreen.

'Gilesy, what are you doing? Where are you?'

'Who is that?' Hope asked, not used to having people interrupt her time talking to her Uncle Giles.

'You know who that is. It's your Aunty Sienna.'

'Aunty Sienna?' The surprise in Hope's voice matched perfectly the somersault in Holly's stomach. Aunty? When had

Giles started referring to Sienna as Aunty? Never in her presence and by the look of confusion on Hope's face, she didn't know who he was talking about either. But before Holly could comment, Sienna's face appeared on the screen behind him.

'Oh, Holly,' she said. 'It's you. How are you?'

A low buzz rolled through Holly's jaw as her back teeth ground together. She tried to force a smile.

'Good morning, Sienna. We're fine, thank you. Hope just wanted to check in on the patient.'

Sienna leaned forward, kissing Giles on the top of the head before she spoke.

'Oh well, he's doing fine. Just fine, and we are looking forward to Friday night, aren't we? Giles has told me all about the wedding. It sounds like it was such a magical event. Hopefully, you'll all have some more stories about the day. I love wedding stories, don't you?'

The muscles in Holly's cheeks were starting to ache from the strain of holding her smile in place. Was Sienna serious? Did she not know her personal wedding story? Or lack thereof?

She drew in a slow breath, readying herself with a curt, yet reasonable reply. But before she could get a word out, Sienna was speaking again.

'Well, we better get on with things. Thank you so much for calling to check on us. Hope, see you soon.' Sienna offered a short wave. A moment later, the phone line was dead.

'Wow, she seemed nice,' Hope said.

7

It was irrational how much two words could play on Holly's mind. For the entire weekend and the following week, they dominated her thoughts. No matter how hard she tried to forget about them. *Aunty Sienna.* Sometimes, she would ruminate on them properly. It was clearly the medication that had caused Giles to say such a thing. Confusion caused by the pain he was in. That was the conclusion she would always come to in such moments, but at other times, she was preoccupied with something entirely different – work, Hope, driving – and Giles's voice would echo in her ear again. The two words would resonate around in Holly's head and refuse to shift, regardless of how much she had to get on with.

He'd never designated any of his other girlfriends 'Aunty' before. Was it a sign? Were things perhaps more serious between him and Sienna than she had realised? Every time the thought arose, she would battle to quash it. Of course that wasn't the case. They were only a few months in. Even when he and Joanna had passed the year mark, Hope and the other children still called her JoJo. It was the painkillers. She was sure. After all, she had spoken to him several times during the week and he hadn't even mentioned her in those conversations.

As Friday rolled around, Holly finally made peace with the slip of the tongue, although she was still terrified Jamie was going to hold her to her word and make her sit next to Sienna for the meal. Fingers crossed, Sienna had been called away for one of her fancy charity functions that she constantly name-dropped about. While Holly wasn't exactly sure what Sienna's role involved, she knew it was a lot more fancy – and substantially better paid – than your standard volunteering job.

'Right, you are not allowed to stay up past eight thirty, do you hear me?' Holly said as she slipped on her dress. 'And you need to stop playing games at seven as well. Tim and Izzy are in charge and they're going to put a film on for you guys to watch. You need to listen to them. If they tell you to do something, you do it. Without fuss. They're in charge. Hope, are you listening? Put that down, please. What did I just say?'

'You said Tim and Izzy are in charge and I have to do what they say.'

'And you're not allowed to stay up late, either. Remember?'

'I know,' Hope said with a groan.

Holly knew what a great kid Hope was, but she also knew how much mischief she could get into when she was with her friends, so a little reminder never hurt.

'Just be sensible, that's all I'm asking. You know how much the twins look up to you. Randall too. I want you to set a good example.'

'I will. I promise. If anyone misbehaves, I will sort it out.'

'You mean you'll let Tim and Izzy sort it out?' Holly corrected.

'Exactly. Yes, of course that's what I meant.'

With a light chuckle, Holly planted a kiss on the top of her daughter's head.

Hope was only in Year Three but had already been voted class counsellor twice. It was probably because of her extreme organisation and willingness to get stuck into any situation, but Holly also wondered how much Hope had coerced her class-mates into voting for her. While both Holly and Ben were people pleasers who hated to cause any form of discord or upset, Hope was bold and fearless, and went into every situation ready to give it her all. Regardless of what else was going on around her. It was a confidence that Holly admired greatly, although she sometimes wished Hope would rein it in a little at home.

When Holly was dressed, she headed next door to find Jamie giving her boys the same talk. There was no doubt that every child knew exactly what their parents' expectations were. Whether they stuck to them would be another matter entirely.

'Did you see the necklace Fin got me for our anniversary?' Jamie said, as they walked down into the village. 'He made it himself, obviously.'

'Obviously.' Holly laughed. She had long since learned that there wasn't anything Fin couldn't do if he put his mind to it. Apparently, that now included ironwork.

'I feel bad. I just got him a card. He said we shouldn't worry about presents this year.'

'He says that every year,' Holly reminded her. 'And then he always gets you something.'

'I know,' Jamie said with a groan. 'But I'm not going to fall for it again. I've already looked it up. It's copper. I have a full year to source the best copper cooking pans I can.'

'Nothing like being prepared.'

'Of course, I'll probably have a couple too many drinks tonight and forget about it entirely, so you're going to have to remind me.'

'Deal.' Holly laughed.

'What are you talking about?' Fin said as he came jogging up behind them. 'Not me, I take it?'

'As if we'd ever talk about you,' Jamie said, reaching up and pecking him on the cheek.

As far as relationship role models went, Holly knew she couldn't do much better than her friends. There were no concerns about their relationship. No worries, no uncertainties. Jamie could start preparing Fin's anniversary present a year in advance because she knew, without a doubt, they would still be together. It was the same for Michael and Caroline, and Ben and Georgia too. It was the same way for her parents and for those brief but wonderful years, how she and Evan had been. But would she ever feel that way again? The older she got, the less likely it felt.

All her friends had spoken to her more than once about moving on. About at least thinking about dating again, but she couldn't. She couldn't risk losing anybody else. Besides, she had all the company and support she could ever hope for. Why would she ever need anybody more?

8

Each year, they went to the same restaurant to celebrate Jamie and Fin's anniversary. It was the one in the centre of the village, where he had celebrated her birthday by hanging hundreds of paper cranes from the ceiling. It was obviously a place with great sentimental meaning for Fin, although for Holly, it was the place where Michael had let slip to everybody that she was pregnant with Ben's baby. At the time, it hadn't felt like good news at all, considering the pair of them had just split up. But now she found something comforting about coming back at the same time every year and seeing how different her life was from how she thought it was going to end up all those years ago.

What had felt like a disaster in the making had turned out to be the best thing in the entire world. Hope. Sometimes, when the darkness and loneliness crept in and she stretched her arm across the double bed, wishing that Evan's body was still there, warming the other side, Holly would think of that night. Her dislike of Fin and her fear of her unborn child, and it would remind her that you could never tell how life was going to turn out. It also reminded her that she'd had a love before Evan, and that maybe, just maybe, it would be possible to have one after him too. Just not yet.

When Holly, Jamie and Fin pushed through the door into the restaurant, they discovered they were the last to arrive. Caroline and Michael were already at the bar talking to Ben, whilst Giles was sitting down at their table with Georgia, and already nursing a large glass of wine.

Holly had spoken to Giles several times on the phone this week, but they hadn't had any more video calls. The last time she'd seen him in person was at the hospital and though she wouldn't have thought it was possible, he looked worse. His bruises had turned a sickly greeny yellow and spread all the way around his face while the bandage on his nose had been removed, showing the extent of the swelling. The cut on his head, however, seemed to be healing, but it was difficult to tell, due to the country-style flat cap he had pulled down over his forehead in a failed attempt to disguise what a state he was in.

'Oh my God, you look terrible,' Jamie said, cutting past Holly to give Giles a tentative hug. 'I didn't realise it was this bad. I'm amazed you came out.'

'Good to see you too.' Giles smirked.

'You know what I mean. How are you doing?'

'It's all right,' Giles said with a shrug. 'It hurts a lot less than it did, anyway. And thankfully, I've had Sienna at my beck and call, being a perfect nurse.'

A high-pitched, nasal laugh rattled up behind Holly.

'Oh, I wouldn't say that. Just doing my best.'

As always, Sienna was dressed immaculately, but rather than her clothes, it was her height that stunned Holly the most. Six-inch heels, added to her already impressive five feet ten, meant that she towered over almost all of them. And with her cascading, blue, mini dress, she looked like she belonged on a runway, not a little country restaurant.

Several judgements ran through Holly's mind, but she stopped herself mid-thought. They weren't justified. She was just being catty, and that wasn't who she wanted to be. With her focus on all the reminders Jamie and Fin had given her, and forcing herself to keep an open mind, Holly smiled broadly.

'Sienna,' she said. 'It's sounds like you've been doing an amazing job. I'm sure he hasn't been the easiest patient.'

Before Holly could say any more, Sienna stepped forwards and then, without warning, engulfed Holly in a hug, squeezing so tightly, Holly thought she might crack a rib. Whatever greeting she had expected from Sienna, this definitely wasn't it, and when she was finally released, she found herself at a loss for words. Sienna, however, already had some prepared.

'Holly, I'm so sorry,' she said. 'I need to apologise before I do anything else. I was so rude to you at the hospital the other day. Can you ever forgive me?'

Stunned didn't come close to how Holly felt at this declaration, but Sienna still wasn't done. 'It was the shock, you know? I guess seeing Giles like that terrified me, and then to add his sister into the mix... I'm ever so sorry. I hope we might be able to sit together during the dinner. I haven't had much of a chance to get to know you properly and I would hate for you to use last week to build an impression of me.'

Holly couldn't look away from Sienna. She knew it would be incredibly rude if she did, but then she didn't need to. Even from where she was standing with her back to her best friend, she could feel the smirk on Jamie's face. There was no way out of it now.

Trying not to show how large an inhalation she needed, Holly coaxed her face into a smile and replied, 'That would be lovely.'

9

'Honestly, Giles talks about you so much,' Sienna said as she picked up the jug of water on the table and promptly filled Holly's glass. 'And Hope. Do you know he's very protective of you both? He thinks of you as family.'

'Yes, well, we've been through a lot.'

Rather than respond, Sienna picked up her wineglass and took a long sip.

'He told me about his past,' Sienna said, an unusual look of seriousness on her face. 'About the things he did with the sweet shop when you first took over the place. Some other things he did too, involving Ben and Jamie. He sounds like he was quite a different person then.'

'He was,' Holly said in surprise.

Giles's wayward past was common knowledge among the group, and they would regularly rib him for it, commenting on how they needed to be careful in case he returned to his traitorous ways. But they were friends. The lack of scruples with which he had gone through his early adulthood hardly seemed like something he'd talk to a stranger about, but then Holly reminded herself that Sienna wasn't exactly a stranger. They were dating. Still, the relationship was obviously more serious than Holly had realised if he was telling her about those things. Those words, *Aunty Sienna*, sprung back into her mind, but before she could dwell on them, Sienna was talking again.

'Hope is just adorable. I think that every time I see her. And now Giles has said that she's got a lead part in the upcoming school concert?'

'Well, I'm not sure I'd call it a lead part,' Holly replied. 'But she is playing the ukulele, and she does have to sing a solo line too.'

'You must tell me all about it.'

By the time the main courses arrived, Holly had spent more time talking to Sienna one on one than in all their other meetings put together. Fin was right about her charity work. The passion with which she spoke about her job implied it wasn't quite the frivolous activity that Holly had previously envisioned, even though during their conversation, she named four celebrities and countless swanky venues. And as silly as it was in comparison, Sienna appeared genuinely enthused by Holly's own charity work for a local care home.

'I don't visit as much as I used to,' Holly said with a pang of guilt. 'To be honest, after Verity passed away, I didn't go in for a long time. I found it too difficult. But over the last couple of years, I've been making more of an effort. I've taken Hope in a couple of times too, and hopefully, we can build that up as she gets older.'

'Oh yes, that would be a wonderful experience for her, I'm sure.'

Conversation passed around the table as they enjoyed their main courses, including countless anecdotes about Jamie and Fin's wedding.

'And Evan's guitar solo,' Caroline said, shaking her head. 'Of course, he could play the guitar. He could do everything.'

'Yes, had we known he was going to steal the spotlight, we'd have just let him be part of the band,' Michael said. 'Actually, no, we wouldn't. He would have shown us all up.'

The group laughed. Including Holly.

For a long time, Evan's name hadn't been mentioned in situations like this. The group had shied away from talking about him at all, as if saying his name would be enough to bring all the memories and heartbreak flooding back to Holly. But the heartbreak was always there. The wound hadn't healed, and she knew now it never could. But speaking about him helped keep him a little more present in her mind.

After the waiter had taken their dessert orders, Holly cleared her throat.

'If you'll excuse me, Sienna, I'm just going to head to the ladies'.'

'Oh, I'll come with you,' Sienna said, placing her napkin on the table in front of her, but before either of them could move, Giles had stood up and clinked his knife against his glass.

'Hi, everybody, just while we're waiting for our desserts, I wanted to say a few words.'

10

All eyes were on Giles, although he didn't get the immediate silence he was probably expecting.

'Have you not had enough attention already this week?' Michael said, lifting his glass and laughing at his own humour.

'Probably,' Giles said. 'But I'm taking the limelight for a minute longer. Sorry.'

He smiled broadly as he looked around the table, before bringing his gaze to a stop at Jamie and Fin.

'So obviously, the first thing I need to do is say a massive congratulations to these guys.'

A cheer went up that was so loud, several other tables looked in their direction. Most of it came from Holly and Caroline, though, and from the way Giles lifted his glass, it was clear he wanted to say more. Only when the noise had subsided did he continue.

'You guys really are the epitome of an amazing couple,' he said. 'You are the most generous people I know. You're doing a phenomenal job of raising three incredible little people and you make being married look easy. I won't lie, I aspire for a relationship as solid as yours, but to be honest, if I end up with a fraction of what you guys have, I would consider that a very successful marriage indeed. So first I want to raise a toast. To Jamie and Fin.'

Glasses rose and a series of cheers followed, this time even louder and longer than the previous one.

'To Jamie and Fin,' everybody said, before taking a sip of their drink.

Like everyone else at the table, Holly's attention was on Jamie and Fin as she lifted her glass. In a manner that was ever so familiar and yet intimate, Fin was whispering something in Jamie's ear, but rather than giggling, or slapping him playfully like she normally did after such an interaction, Jamie's face tightened. A second later, her gaze spun around to fix on Holly.

What was going on? The elation she had been feeling at her friends' celebration only a second ago was twisting into something uncomfortable, although she didn't understand why. Was Jamie annoyed that Giles had taken over doing the toast? That wasn't the type of thing that normally annoyed her, but something about her expression was off. Everyone else around the table was smiling and clinking glasses as they leaned in towards Jamie and Fin, but even when everyone was done, Giles remained standing. It was a little odd, Holly thought, given that he had made a perfectly good toast. And yet, as he remained standing, his eyes shifted from Jamie and Fin across to where Sienna and Holly were sitting.

'I just want to say one other thing.' As he drew in a breath, his grip tightened on his wineglass. Was he nervous? He certainly looked like it. But why? All Holly could do was wait to see what he was going to say, but it was hard with the way Jamie and Fin's eyes kept darting towards her and every second that passed, they were looking more and more worried. Had something happened? Had they had a call from a babysitter? No, that didn't make sense either. They had a group chat set up for that. So what was going on?

There was no way she could ask now, though. Not with Giles still mid-speech. She would just have to wait until he was done. Then she could find out. Thankfully, Giles was talking again. Fingers crossed, whatever he had to say wouldn't take too long.

'This week, as you know, I had a bit of an accident,' he said. 'You might not be able to tell, because I'm still substantially more attractive than the average person, even with all these bruises and a newly angled nose.'

A series of groans rolled around the table, and Holly noticed a small smile flicker on the corner of Jamie's lips. Maybe she had misread the situation. Maybe it wasn't that bad after all. Either way, she would find out when Giles finally sat down. Unfortunately, he was still going.

'I won't say life flashed before my eyes. And it was my own stupidity that put me in that situation, as some of you have already pointed out.' His gaze flicked to Holly with the slight hint of a smirk she couldn't help but reciprocate, though he had moved on almost immediately. 'It was scary, though. I know that no one around this table takes their future for granted. We've been through too much for that, but strangely, I'm grateful for the accident, because it made me see the important things in life, and the important things are sitting here with me today. You lot. The people I love.'

Holly's heart swelled. Giles had a way with words, particularly when he wasn't using them to gain something for himself. She assumed that another toast was incoming. This time to all of them. Or perhaps even to Evan – it wouldn't be the first time they had toasted his name at dinners like this. She reached for her glass, but instead, Giles said something altogether different.

'So I think this is the moment I've got to move, so I have enough room to kneel down.'

Caroline's hand shot to her mouth in a gasp, while Jamie's eyes darted across to Holly again. But Holly still didn't understand what was going on. Why did he need to kneel down?

She watched him manoeuvre himself out from the table, but rather than kneeling properly, he was just on one knee. That was when she realised what was happening. Giles was proposing to Sienna.

'Any chance you can come round here, sweetie?' he said.

Holly turned to look at Sienna. Her eyes were filled with tears as she struggled to stand. Did tears mean she was going to say yes or no? Surely it would be no. Surely she couldn't think they'd been together long enough to get married?

She was certainly taking a long time moving, and with every step, Holly's mind whirred. If she said no, what would that do to Giles? Would he be humiliated? He couldn't really be serious though, could he? It had to be the painkillers making him act that way. Everyone knew you weren't meant to mix alcohol and painkillers, and that was obviously what he had done. It was just a spur-of-the-moment thing. Sienna would realise that, wouldn't she? But then, as he knelt there, Giles pulled out a small square box. Holly's heart twisted. How spur-of-the-moment could it be if he'd got a ring?

'Okay, I'm gonna make this quick,' Giles said as Sienna reached him. 'Because it's really starting to hurt my muscles now. But Sienna Louisabell Sommercroft...'

Louisabell! Was that even a name?

She wasn't going to voice the question though, and even if she had, she doubted anyone would have heard. They were all transfixed on the scene. Giles, on one knee, with a ring in one hand as he held on to Sienna's with the other.

'You are a truly wonderful person. And I feel so lucky to have you in my life. Would you do me the honour of becoming my wife?'

Sienna used her free hand to cover her mouth as tears streamed down her cheeks. She shook her head. Was that a no? Holly wondered. Maybe it was a no. But a second later, Sienna finally croaked out an answer.

'Yes, yes, absolutely I will.'

The entire table erupted into cheers. Almost the entire table at least. Holly was too stunned to even move.

11

While most of the table was on their feet, heading towards the newly engaged couple. Michael took hold of the champagne bottle and started refilling everyone's glasses, only for the drink to run out after filling just Jamie's and Sienna's.

'More champagne!' He waved his hand energetically as he looked for a member of the waitstaff to fulfil the request. Yet before he could find one, Holly was on her feet.

'I'll go get some more,' Holly said, pushing back her chair as she rose, only to find her legs felt peculiarly weak. 'One more bottle of champagne coming up.'

A moment later, she was walking towards the bar. By the time she got there, not only had her legs failed to regain any of their strength, but her throat was unnaturally dry and an almost dizzy-like sensation was causing her head to spin.

'A glass of water, please,' she said to the barman.

'No problem.' He provided her with one almost immediately, although she couldn't bring herself to take a sip.

'Hey, you okay?'

Holly didn't move. She could feel her hand gripping the glass a little tighter than it needed to. Anger was rising through her, but she tried to keep it in.

'Holly, I said are you okay?'

She spun around. Jamie was only inches away from her.

'How the hell could you let him do that?' she said.

She didn't want to take her feelings out on Jamie. That wasn't fair. She knew it wasn't, but she was angry, and Jamie was the only person there to be the recipient.

'It's your anniversary party. We were celebrating your wedding, and you just let him usurp it like that?'

'I don't think that's what he did,' Jamie said. Her voice was quiet and considered and, for some reason, that only made Holly even more irritated.

'That's completely what he did. I mean, how arrogant can you get? To not even ask someone when you're at their anniversary party. To not even tell them you're going to propose.'

'Well, actually...'

Holly felt her jaw slacken. She shook her head in disbelief.

'He told you? He told you he was going to propose, but you didn't tell me?'

It was Jamie's turn to shake her head. 'He asked if it would be okay and Fin said yes. I only found out a few minutes before you did.'

Holly recalled the look on Jamie's face as Fin whispered in her ear. That was the moment. She realised it now. That was the moment Jamie knew what was going to happen.

'You could have let me know somehow,' she said.

'Really? How? What did you want me to do? Wave across the table and say, "I needed to talk to you about something," just after Fin told me?'

'Well, you could've been more subtle about it than that,' Holly said with a sniff.

With a long sigh, Jamie looked across at the barman, who was on his phone.

'Is he getting the extra champagne?' she said.

'I was just about to order it,' Holly huffed.

'Two more bottles of champagne please.' Jamie gestured to the barman. A moment later, he was filling an ice bucket. 'I know this isn't going to be easy for you,' Jamie said softly, 'but maybe that feeling you're feeling right now is telling you something. Something you haven't really wanted to admit to yourself.'

Holly scoffed. 'You mean that Giles is still the same egocentric arse he always was, having to make every situation about him?'

'No, that isn't what I meant. Holly, surely you can tell it's not normal to be upset that your friends are getting married, right? You wouldn't feel like that if it was Ben and Georgia getting engaged.'

'Of course I wouldn't. They're in an actual relationship. They have children together. It would be entirely different.'

'And you don't think there's another difference here? What with it being Giles and everything.'

It was hard to deny Jamie was right about something. Why was she so angry? Apart from Giles usurping the evening and Sienna being a less than ideal match for him, it was probably the shock, she realised. Shock that she had been the last to know. Fin, Jamie, they all knew before she did, when she was meant to be Giles's best friend. That was what the issue was. That was why she was so freaking angry with him.

'That'll be eighty-eight pounds, please, love,' the barman said, placing a bottle of champagne in a new ice bucket in front of them. 'Do you want to split the cost?'

'No,' Jamie and Holly spoke simultaneously.

'No,' Holly repeated, 'I'll get it. I'll pay for it. The last thing I want is for people to think I'm not pleased for my friend.'

With that, she tapped her card against the machine, picked up the ice bucket and strode back to the table.

12

'Holly, you must look at this ring. It's absolutely stunning, isn't it?'

The moment Holly arrived back at the table with the bottle of champagne, Caroline was there holding Sienna's hand in hers, twisting it up at the wrist, so the diamond that sat on Sienna's ring finger was now facing Holly.

A slight prickling came from behind her eyes, which may or may not have been due to the light shining off said diamond and directly into her eye.

'Wow, yes, that's beautiful,' she said, choking back the feeling that was once again writhing in her stomach.

'It's very cute, that's what it is,' Sienna said. Her smile was unbelievably wide, and she kept wiping her hand against her cheeks, as if she was still having to brush away tears, although it didn't look to Holly like she was crying any more. And somehow, even though the initial bout of tears had been more than a little dramatic, her makeup had stayed perfectly in place. If it had been anyone else, Holly would have asked her what brand of mascara she used, but it didn't feel quite right to say such a thing during what was clearly meant to be an emotional moment. 'I mean, it's really delicate, isn't it? Understated.'

'Absolutely,' Holly said, though Sienna didn't respond. Instead, she held her hand slightly higher before turning her wrist and allowing the light to fall on the stone from all directions.

It was only when Sienna cleared her throat that Holly realised she had been standing there for several minutes more without saying something. But what could she say? She still had dozens of questions rolling through her head. Like when had Giles gone shopping for it? He had said he was staying in last week, to rest up, the way the doctors had told him he needed to do, but did that mean he had bought it before or had he lied to Holly about how he was spending the week? He hadn't mentioned to her that he was planning on buying a ring or even looking at them. Wasn't that the type of thing you'd normally take a best friend with you to do? Especially when that best friend was female?

'You are very, very lucky,' she said as Caroline continued to gush away about things like insurance and checking the setting prongs. 'I hope you don't mind. I'm just gonna go outside to ring the house and check on Hope.'

'Check on Hope?' Caroline asked in surprise as she finally looked away from Sienna. 'Why are you going to do that? She'll be fine. It's not like we haven't been out for dinner before.'

'No, it's just, she was just feeling a little bit unwell when we left,' Holly lied. 'Nothing serious. I think it's nerves about the school performance, so I just want to check in quickly.'

'Oh, well, I do hope she's okay,' Sienna said. 'And don't worry, I'll make sure there's plenty of champagne left.'

'Great. Wonderful,' Holly said.

A moment later, she was walking outside the pub towards the river, unsure why the temperature had suddenly got so hot.

13

Bourton didn't really have an unattractive season. Whether the scenery was the medley of oranges and browns of the trees in the late-summer months, or the lush array of wildflowers that appeared during spring. Even dark, rainy days had their allure about them. But as Holly sat on one of the benches, staring out at the water, the scene felt peculiarly dreary.

'Here you are. I wondered where you got to.'

The voice caused Holly's pulse to spike, though she tried her best to hide it as she fixed a smile on her face.

'I guess congratulations are in order,' she said. 'Marriage? Wow, it's a big step.'

Giles grinned. 'You're telling me. I'm not sure I ever thought this day would come. May I?'

He gestured to the bench, at which point Holly nodded once and shifted herself to the side so there was room for him to sit.

Silence swirled between them. Holly was used to silences with Giles. They could sit for hours next to one another, sometimes reading books, sometimes watching films, sometimes just driving in the car together with one of them gazing out of the window. But this felt different. This felt like a silence when nobody knew what to say.

'So...'

'I want...'

They both spoke simultaneously.

'Sorry,' Giles said, 'you go.'

'No, you...'

'No, honestly...'

Holly took a deep breath in. Now that she had been interrupted, she couldn't actually remember what it was she was going to say. There must have been something she had wanted to tell him, but the words had already escaped her.

'I was just going to say it's a lovely ring,' she said finally. 'Really beautiful.'

That definitely hadn't been what she'd intended on saying before, but it seemed like as good a comment as any. Though rather than reacting with a standard, 'thank you', as she expected, Giles looked at his lap.

'I'm sorry,' he said.

'Sorry?'

'I didn't think about the engagement and you. How it would affect you.'

'Affect me?' Holly said. 'You getting engaged doesn't affect me, Giles.'

He clasped his hands together, pressing his thumbs into his palms as he spoke.

'I mean the engagement itself. You know, because Evan didn't get to give you his ring and there you are seeing me get down on one knee when that never actually happened for you. I'm sorry, I should've thought how painful that must've been. I just got caught up in my own thoughts. Typical Giles, I suppose.' A smile crossed his lips, only to disappear just as quickly as it formed. 'I get it. I get why you needed to go to the bar. Why you needed to come out for some air. I'm sorry I put you in that position.'

Was that why Holly was feeling so put out? Because she had seen Giles propose to Sienna in a manner she would never experience? A manner that had been snatched from her without warning? Maybe that was it. Maybe that explained the hollowness in her stomach.

'It's okay,' Holly said. 'Really, I think it's lovely that you wanted to get us all involved in the day. That made it really special.'

'Thank you. Even if you don't mean it. Thank you for pretending for me.' This time, his smile lasted a fraction longer before once again it faded and a second silence settled. Their gazes drifted out into the water.

'Do you remember when you pushed me in there?' Giles said with a gruff chuckle. 'After you found out what I was doing.'

'Feels like a lifetime ago,' Holly replied.

'Feels like a different life.'

'Well, it was nearly a decade ago. And you're not the same person any more.'

Rather than responding, Giles hummed. 'I hated being him, you know. I hated hurting people. I just thought that was who I had to be to get ahead.' He paused again, but before Holly could respond, he turned to face her. 'It just took you to get it out of me. We both know I wouldn't be who I am.'

Holly sighed. Yet another silence was going to form, but before it did, Giles continued.

'I've been thinking these last couple of days about the wedding and everything, and I know it might be difficult for you, but there's no one else I'd rather ask. But you can say no, if you want.'

'Ask what?' Holly replied, her stomach churning as she tried to imagine what could be coming.

'I was hoping you'd be my best man. Well, best woman.'

'Your best woman?'

Holly wasn't sure how to respond. Giles wanted her to be there, standing by his side, when he got married. When he said his vows to Sienna.

A lump formed in her throat, and she wasn't entirely sure why. But before she could respond, Giles was on his feet.

'Sorry, it's too much to put this on you right now... but think about it, will you? There's honestly no one else I'd want with me. After all, I don't think I'd have become marriage material without your help. You will think about it though, won't you?'

Holly nodded, not sure what else she could do.

'Of course,' she said. 'Of course I will.'

14

Holly couldn't have been truer to her word when it came to thinking about Giles's offer. She thought about it as she walked back to the table with yet another bottle of champagne, and as everyone lavished their congratulations on Sienna and Giles. She thought about it as she made her way home and as she checked on Hope, fast asleep in Jamie's house. And when she headed back to hers alone, it was the same thought rolling over and over in her head.

'It's really not that big a deal,' she said, looking at Rhubarb as she spoke. The kitten had been sound asleep when Holly came home, but as soon as she had turned on the tap to get herself a glass of water, she had woken up and bounded across to her. Several minutes of fuss and strokes had followed, but now she was wrestling with one of Holly's shoelaces. 'It's good news. It shows he's grown up. Now, enough about that. What do you say we do some baking together? Not that you can eat any of it.'

While the cat continued to writhe about on the floor, Holly opened up the cupboards and scoured the contents. There was flour and sugar and she was bound to have some eggs somewhere. Baking felt like a natural thing to do, even though it was nearly midnight. For whatever reason, she was wide awake and the last thing she wanted was to lie in bed, staring up at the ceiling in an empty house with her mind on overdrive. And nothing calmed her mind like baking.

Ten minutes later, Holly slipped a batch of blueberry muffins into the oven. Now all she had to do was wait for them to bake, and given how late it was in the UK, she knew the perfect way to pass the time.

'Hey, you,' Holly said, as her video call was answered in one ring. 'Is now a good time?'

'Sure thing, sis. How are you doing?'

Erin wasn't actually Holly's sister-in-law, or related to her in any way. But had Evan still been alive, and the pair of them married the way they hoped, then she would've been one of the four sisters-in-law that Holly gained, two of whom were identical triplets.

Holly and Erin's relationship didn't get off to the best start, although if you're meeting someone for the first time after a mutually beloved person's death, it's hardly likely to be the best situation. While Holly was refusing to admit grief, Erin had been wanting to find blame wherever she could, and so directed it straight at Holly. Somehow, though, the pair had made it through those times and come out the other side as firm friends. In fact, Holly had now reached the point where she spoke to Erin even more than she did Evan's parents, who continued to view Hope as one of their own grandchildren and made sure they rang for a minimum of weekly updates.

'Where's my favourite English niece?' Erin said, before shaking her head. 'Sorry, I forgot about the time. I'm guessing she's in bed, right?'

'She is,' Holly replied, 'though she's staying at Jamie's tonight. I've got the house to myself.'

'Great, let me guess, you're on a late-night television binge, right?' Erin grinned.

'Not exactly.' Holly tried to smile back, but her muscles were unusually slow to reciprocate the action. When she finally managed, it was too late.

'What's going on?' Erin said. 'Something's up.'

'No, no, not at all,' Holly said. 'Just a busy evening, that's all. Busy and unexpected.'

Erin arched an eyebrow. 'Is that right? Why? What happened? Spill all the goss.'

'Well, it's not goss, really.' The knot that formed in the pit of her stomach earlier in the evening was now reforming. 'It's just that – I don't know – it's good news, I guess. Giles proposed to his girlfriend Sienna. Giles is getting married.'

Erin's face was a picture. Her jaw dropped so far, Holly could almost see the back of her throat.

'Giles? Your Giles?'

'He's not my Giles,' Holly said defensively. 'He's Sienna's Giles.'

'Well, is he? I thought you two were inseparable?'

Holly chewed on the inside of her cheek. 'Giles and I are just friends – you know that. We've always been friends.'

'Well yes, but...'

'But what?'

Erin rolled her lips several times before she offered a non-committal shrug. 'I don't know, I guess he was just hanging on until...'

'Hanging on for what?' Holly said.

Erin shook her head and let out a slight sigh before fixing a smile back onto her face.

'Hey, what do I know? I live on the other side of the world. This is exciting, yes? I guess you're gonna be involved in the planning?'

'Apparently, he wants me to be his best woman.'

'Best woman?'

'Best man, only I'm a woman.'

'Wow, big responsibility. How do you feel about that?'

Confused. That was how Holly felt. Confused as to whether she wanted that role and confused as to why she felt so confused. She was the obvious choice, after all. Even ahead of Ben or Fin, she and Giles were closest, but it still felt peculiar to be asked such a thing. She opened her mouth, ready to say as much to Erin, when a loud ringing cut through from the other end of the phone.

'Sorry!' Erin said quickly, standing up. 'I invited Mel and Ashley and the kids over. They're always late, so I thought I had time to chat to you, but we need to pause this conversation, okay? I don't want you doing anything you're uncomfortable with, even if it's for your best mate. All right? I'll ring you soon, and you can tell me how you feel about this. How you really feel. Gotta go, though. Love you.'

'Love you too,' Holly responded, yet before she had finished, the phone line was dead.

15

It wasn't the most restful night's sleep. The knot in Holly's stomach refused to loosen, and every time she felt herself drifting off, another intrusive thought would cause a spike in anxiety. She wasn't even sure why it was happening. The way her pulse would suddenly rise, or her breathing become painfully shallow, wasn't something she'd ever really suffered from before. Not without good reason, anyway.

Unsurprisingly, she'd had trouble sleeping after Evan passed away, and the doctor had given her sleeping tablets, which she'd taken now and then when she really needed to, but it had been so long since the last time she'd felt them necessary, she wasn't even sure if she had any in the house. So why would it have come back all of a sudden? There was no reason for her to be feeling anxious about anything, was there? Unless, of course, it was the thought of messing up the important role that Giles had given her. Maybe it was that. Maybe that was the reason she hadn't been able to respond. Not because she didn't want to do it, but because she was worried she wouldn't do a good enough job.

Of course, it didn't help that Rhubarb repeatedly wanted to

play. It felt like every time Holly started to drift off, the cat would decide to use her body for pouncing practice, but there was no point shutting her out. If she did that, she knew she'd just spend the entire night listening to the kitten whining and scratching at the door.

Strangely, it was a relief when morning finally came around and she didn't have to try to sleep any more. Instead, with her pyjamas still on, she headed around the back of the house and let herself in through Jamie's back door into the kitchen.

'What time are you working at the shop today?' Jamie asked as she moved towards the coffee machine with three mugs: hers, Fin's and Holly's too. It really was a special type of friendship when you had your own mug at their house.

'Not until midday. Greta's running it until then.' The new member of staff had come with a wealth of employment history and was as capable as both Caroline and Holly of running things by themselves. 'Any sign of my daughter yet?'

Jamie shook her head. 'I think she's still fast asleep. By the sounds of it, they had a pretty late night. I figured I'd give them another half an hour, then wake them up.'

'Sounds good.'

Holly took the mug of coffee from Jamie and perched herself at the breakfast bar where she proceeded to blow the steam from the top.

'So, do you want to talk about last night?' Jamie said. 'You seemed to have a pretty visceral reaction.'

'Visceral? That's a big word to use.'

'What would you rather I said: emotional?'

Holly pouted as she took a sip of her drink. 'Of course it was emotional. I was surprised. I didn't get the early warning that you did.'

With a resigned sigh, Jamie shook her head. 'You're not really going on about that, are you? I didn't get an early warning, and it wouldn't have changed things even if I did. And you're still avoiding answering the question.'

'That's because there's no question to answer.'

'Yes, there is. How do you feel?'

'How do I feel?' Holly shrugged. She really didn't have any idea what Jamie was expecting her to say on the matter, but the line of questioning felt unusually intrusive, and considering they had both seen one another in labour, that was saying something. 'How do you think I'm feeling? Giles is getting married. I'm happy for him.'

'Really?'

'Of course, really. Just like I'll be happy when Ben finally gets round to proposing to Georgia.'

Ben and Georgia had been together for six years now and had two beautiful children together. Hope's siblings. They were, by all accounts, a perfect couple, which was why Holly always found it strange that Ben hadn't yet asked her to marry him. Georgia definitely seemed like the type of woman who would want a wedding.

'It's a bit different, though, isn't it?' Jamie said.

'Is it? Why?' Holly asked. 'You mean because Ben and I were in a relationship together? Does that mean I should have a more or less visceral reaction?'

Holly couldn't help but smirk, even though she knew how childish she was being.

'All I'm saying is I'm here to talk about things. If you want to talk about them. That's all.'

'Good,' Holly replied. 'Because I might actually need you to.'

'You might?' Jamie put her cup down and leaned forward on the chair. 'I knew it.'

'Giles has named me his best woman, which means I'm in

charge of the stag do and the speeches, and whatever else he puts me in charge of.'

'He has?' Jamie said. 'And you've agreed to do it?'

'Of course I have. Why wouldn't I?' Holly wasn't sure why she'd lied. If she wanted to talk to about feeling apprehensive, then Jamie was probably her best bet, but for some reason, she wanted to keep her doubts to herself. But now that the lie was out, she felt the need to double down. 'I'm sure it'll be great fun. Even if it is a lot of work.'

With a twitch tightening in her jawline, Jamie stood back up straight again, while looking Holly dead in the eye.

'Well, I guess you know exactly what you're doing,' she said.

16

After half an hour of talking, the children finally ambled downstairs and Holly found herself faced with a very sleepy Hope.

'Did someone stay up a bit too late?' Holly said as she hoisted Hope up onto her hips. She was far too large to pick up in such a manner now and it would only be a couple of years until she was as tall as Holly, but at that point, she wouldn't be able to pick her up at all, and Holly was determined to make the most of it. Yawning loudly, Hope nestled her head into Holly's shoulder.

'It was Randall's fault,' she said. 'He wanted to watch the film.'

'Is that right?' Holly exchanged a look with Jamie. 'Because I'm sure you said you were the one who wanted to watch something.'

'No, it wasn't me,' Hope insisted, but she couldn't even get the words out before yawning again.

Moments like this, when Hope wanted nothing more than to snuggle, were enough to make Holly's heart swell. It was impossible to think that one day, she'd be a grown woman who didn't need her mum for anything at all, although fingers crossed she'd still want cuddles even then.

'Well, how about we go home, give you a bath, and snuggle Rhubarb before Mummy has to go to the shop?'

'I want to play.'

'Okay, you can play,' Holly said, although she could already see the way her morning was panning out: Hope asleep on the sofa with Rhubarb curled up next to her. Still, there were worse ways to spend a day.

As it happened, after half an hour of dozing and a big, warm bubble bath, during which she created a variety of 'potions', Hope was raring to get outside in the garden and practise her cartwheels.

Holly sat with a book and a kitten on her lap as she watched her daughter until just after eleven, when the doorbell went.

'Hope, that'll be your dad. Go upstairs and get your things please, sweetie. I'll let him in.'

'But I've nearly got it!' Hope said, stamping her foot on the ground. It was a sure sign that the tiredness was still there, lingering beneath the surface. Any second now, she was going to crash.

'You can practise your cartwheels at Daddy's, Hope. I'm sure Ivy and Grace would like to see how well you do them now.'

Mentioning her sisters was the one thing that got Hope moving.

'Fine,' she said, striding towards the house. 'But I need to take all my bunnies. I don't like sleeping without having them all.'

'Then you better go pack them.'

A minute later, Holly was opening the front door, while Hope was stomping her way up the stairs.

'She's exhausted,' Holly said, as she stepped to the side and let Ben into the house. 'I don't know what kind of mood she's going to be in later. Just so you're forewarned.'

'It's fine,' Ben said. 'She'll cheer up when she sees the girls. They've been trying to make me come and fetch her since they woke up.'

Holly smiled. As an only child, she often felt in awe of the love Hope shared with her siblings, and it was a bond she suspected would only grow as they got older.

'She's getting her teddies sorted, which means she'll be a while. Want a cup of coffee?'

'Tea would be great,' he replied. 'And can I smell blueberry muffins?'

Holly couldn't help but laugh.

'Come on through. I'll put some in a tub and you can take them back for the others.'

'So,' Ben said as he followed her into the kitchen. 'Last night was a bit of a surprise. For me, anyway. I assume you knew it was going to happen.'

'No,' Holly said, grateful she had her back to Ben so he couldn't see her face. 'No, I didn't know it was going to happen. So, yes. It was a definitely a surprise.'

'But a good one, right?'

What was it with people using that tone with her? Why would people not think Giles getting married was a good thing? Other than he had completely rushed into it, and Sienna was the worst match possible and it was bound to end in disaster. Thinking about it like that, it was no surprise people wanted to talk about it, although for Holly, a different topic of conversation was taking priority in her mind. There was a question she wanted to ask. One she had thought countless times over the last few years, but never said. Yet, as she began to fill a plastic tub with the previous night's baking, she knew she couldn't keep it in any longer. Stopping what she was doing, she turned around and looked at Ben.

'I need to ask you something,' she said. 'Is that all right?'

'Sure. Go ahead – what is it?'

Holly took a deep breath in as she considered if she actually wanted to do this. In the end, though, it wasn't about wants. It really did feel like a need. So, with an apologetic smile already forming on her lips, she locked eyes with Ben.

'I want to know why you've never proposed to Georgia,' she said.

17

It was a surprising relief to finally get that question out. After all, she had probably thought about it over a hundred times in the last few years.

Rather than replying immediately with a throwaway answer, Ben stared down at his coffee. Holly wasn't surprised by this response. Ben was always thoughtful about how he replied to questions and with this being of such a personal nature – and also involving Georgia – she knew he would want to answer with care.

Still, as the pause expanded, she couldn't happen but wonder if she had made a mistake. She and Ben were incredibly open with others, discussing every aspect of Hope's life and welfare together, but they had an unspoken boundary when it came to Georgia and the girls. Beyond Hope, that part of his life wasn't any of Holly's business yet, for the first time, it felt like she might have crossed that boundary.

'It's just that last night made me think about it, I guess,' she said, growing acutely aware of the silence that was sweeping between them. 'You've got two children together, a house together. You're a perfect couple. I can't believe it's just wanting to save money. But... I mean, it's nothing to do with me. If you don't want to say...'

Ben lifted his thumb to his mouth, momentarily bit down on the nail, before he looked up at Holly.

'Do you want to know the truth?' he said finally.

She frowned. 'Of course I do. That's why I asked.'

Once again, Ben didn't reply. Instead, he drew in a long breath, which he blew out again far slower than felt normal. Almost as if he was nervous. An undeniable churning took hold of Holly, though she didn't understand why.

'So, I did propose,' he said.

'What?' Holly shook her head in disbelief. 'You mean... You mean she said no? What? I don't get it. You two are so happy.'

A smile flickered on Ben's lips, although it didn't match his eyes. Those were uncharacteristically sad.

'I proposed on a lovely, snowy weekend, just before Christmas. Five years ago.'

'Five years ago?' The realisation was like a mallet to her chest, emptying the air from her lungs. Her hands flew up to cover her mouth. 'Oh my God.'

'I shouldn't have said anything,' Ben said, reaching across for her. With her hands trembling, Holly shook him away, not because she was cross, though. Because she couldn't believe she didn't know.

'You proposed to her? The same weekend? And you didn't say anything?'

He shrugged, and that same sadness glinted in his eyes.

'It wasn't a planned proposal. We were looking in the window of a shop and Georgia saw a ring she liked, so I suggested we buy it. Probably not a proposal by most people's standards at all.'

'Wow.' It was the only word Holly could manage. However he

tried to dismiss it, it was a proposal. She suspected Ben had walked Georgia past the ring shop deliberately for that reason: so he didn't have to risk buying the wrong thing. It was a very sensible, very Ben proposal.

'Why didn't you say anything?' Holly said, finally finding her voice again. Yet as Ben tilted his head to the side, another thought hit her. 'You came to America! You came to America with me, days after you proposed.'

'Of course I did. You needed me.'

Tears welled in Holly's eyes. She'd heard so many people say that you only got one great love of your life, but as far as non-romantic love went, she couldn't imagine feeling more for a person than she did for Ben in that moment.

'Surely you could've asked again?' she said. 'Have you asked again?'

Ben reached across the table, placing his hands on hers.

'What happened with Evan made us see that what matters is each other. That's it. We know we'll spend the rest of our lives growing old together and making amazing memories. We don't need an extravagant day to prove that to anyone.' His face suddenly flushed. 'Not that there's anything wrong with that, of course. Marriage is wonderful; I'm not saying it isn't. And we've discussed it – how maybe we would like to wait until the girls are a bit older so they can join in. So that it can be a day everyone remembers. That idea feels even more special to us. Does that make sense?'

'It does,' Holly said. 'Completely.'

She shifted her gaze back down to the table. To the diamond ring that felt even more fraudulent than when she had first put it on. There was nothing more she could say. She had wanted an answer to a question, and now she had it.

'Should I have told you?' Ben said. 'I'm worried now that I shouldn't have told you. It's just that—'

'No, no, I'm so grateful you did,' Holly said. 'Really, I am. I just feel terrible. I feel like I've stopped you two from living your lives.'

'What?' Ben shook his head. 'That's not what happened at all. What happened with you just made us see things differently, that's all. I promise you have absolutely nothing to feel guilty for.'

Holly nodded. Of course he would say that, and he probably meant it too.

'Do the others know?' she asked. 'Jamie? Giles?'

Ben shook his head. 'No, we hadn't even told our parents before we found out about the accident. We wanted to have some time together first. But I think maybe fate played a part in our thinking there too.'

'Maybe,' Holly said, though she wasn't a great believer in fate any more.

She noticed several small droplets of water on the table by her fingers, realising her tears were falling freely now, but as she moved to wipe them away, a voice rang out from the hallway.

'Why are you two just sitting there? I need to go and practise my cartwheels!'

Holly jolted out of her seat, hastily turning so that her back was to Hope while she wiped her tears away. A moment later, she forced a smile onto her lips as she turned back to face her daughter.

'So you're ready at last,' she said.

Hope was standing in the doorway, a large rucksack on her back, the zip not yet done up as it overspilled with teddies. 'Come on,' she said. 'I haven't got all day!'

And as he stood up, Ben's eyes remained solely on Holly.

'Are you going to be all right?' he said. 'Not just about this, about last night too. Are you all right with everything?'

'Of course,' Holly said, throwing back her head and smiling far too energetically to be believable. 'I'm absolutely fine. With everything. Now, you two need to get going. I've got a sweet shop to run, you know.'

18

Holly couldn't remember the last time her mind had felt so full. How could she have gone half a decade and not known about Ben and Georgia? Though now she knew, it made perfect sense. They had been dating longer than she and Evan and had just moved into his house only a couple of months before. She should have seen the signs, only she was too wrapped up in her own life.

And then there was the way everyone kept asking her if she was okay about Giles and Sienna, like being the only single person left in the group would somehow push her over a ledge, even though she'd been the only single person in the group for years. If you could consider Giles's constant string of flings.

Thankfully, the sweet shop was having one of its busiest days of the year, meaning she had little time to focus on it all.

By the time it got to five o'clock, she turned the sign on the door to *Closed* and let out a deep sigh.

It had been a fudge day. Some days were just like that, where one item sold substantially more than any other. There had been days where she'd sold out of sherbet lemons, or chocolate-covered honeycomb. And she recalled one summer where she had to order three times the number of marzipan teacakes because they just kept selling out. But today it was fudges of all flavours: white chocolate meringue, dark chocolate orange, crumbly Scottish-style tablet and even the little coconut-covered fudge rolls. It felt like every customer had purchased several bags of the sweet, and she knew she was going to have to place another order earlier than normal.

Wanting to get the job done as soon as possible, she returned to the counter and pulled out her laptop, when there was a knock on the door.

Her muscles clenched slightly; she hated turning customers away, but she really needed to get on with all the tasks she had to do. So plastering her best smile on her face, she moved back to the door, ready to apologise and say they were closed. Only it wasn't a customer standing there, wanting to come in. Although as a sinking feeling formed in Holly's stomach, she wished it had been.

'Any chance we can talk for two minutes?' Giles said.

Even as her throat turned inexplicably dry, Holly knew there was no way she could say no. Giles regularly turned up after work like this, just to sit and chat, and while away the time. Sometimes, he gave Holly a lift home afterwards, or they'd go for a walk around the village too. If she was busy, he normally just waited, responding to emails on his phone, or sometimes helping her restock the shelves so she could finish a little quicker. Not once had she told him to get lost, meaning there was no way she could do so now without appearing like something was wrong. And nothing was wrong. Was it?

'Hey, of course,' she said. He quickly stepped inside before she closed the door and locked it behind him. 'Do you need something? Only I need to get a fudge order sent off before I go. The busloads of tourists practically wiped me out.'

'No, everything is good,' Giles said. 'Everything is good. Only, I wanted to apologise again. For the way I sprung that on you. I didn't mean it to be such a surprise.'

'I think that's the point of proposals,' Holly said, as she went back to the counter and opened her laptop. 'They're meant to be a surprise.'

For some reason, she was finding it harder than normal to meet Giles's gaze, but it was probably because she still had so much to do before she could head home. If he'd just comes to repeat what he said to her out by the river last night, then it didn't feel like it was the most productive use of either of their time.

'I know it was meant to be a surprise for Sienna, but people usually talk through these things with their friends first, don't they?'

'Do they? I don't think so. It was your proposal. You got to do it however you wanted to.'

'Oh, okay then.' He paused and shifted his position a couple of times. It was like his feet couldn't get comfortable on the floor. Either that, or he was nervous. But Giles didn't do nervous. 'So, we're all right, aren't we? You and I, this doesn't change anything between us? We're fine, right?'

The word 'yes' filled Holly's mind. That was the word she was meant to say. Yes, they were fine. She was fine, she was better than fine. She was happy that Giles had found someone he wanted to spend the rest of his life with. She was excited for the future he'd obviously mapped out in his mind and looking forward to helping him plan for those days. Those were the words she knew she was supposed to say to him, just like she'd said out by the river only minutes after he'd popped the question, but instead of that simple, single-syllable word she knew she was meant to say, what actually came out of her mouth was a question.

'Why her?' she said. 'Why Sienna?'

19

The moment the question left her mouth, she regretted it. To start with, Giles had expected an answer, not another question. Second, it was none of her business. But as he tilted his head to the side, and a frown crinkled his forehead, she knew she was going to get a response. Whether she liked it would be another matter.

'What do you mean?' he said. 'Sienna and I have been together for eight months now.'

'Exactly, and you were with Joanna for fourteen. You were with Kaylee for ten. Why Sienna? Why is she the one you're choosing to spend the rest of your life with? What's different about her? What's special?'

Giles bit down on his bottom lip before he spoke.

'You're saying you don't like her? Is that what you're saying?'

'No, I think she is perfectly pleasant—'

'Perfectly pleasant. Wow, that really is a compliment.'

Holly's temperature was rising and she could feel her back teeth grinding together, but she would not lose her cool. She refused to.

'Well, what do you expect me to say? You haven't answered my question yet, have you? I just wanted to know.'

'Why Sienna. Yes, I heard you. I don't know. It just felt like the right time to make this decision. I'm nearly forty, Holly, and with everything that happened, I realised I needed to think about the future. Properly for once.'

Holly scoffed, then shook her head, lifting her hands in the air.

'So what you're basically saying is that you had an accident, suddenly feared your mortality and decided that's it. I'm going to propose before I get too old.'

'When you put it like that, it sounds horrendous.'

'It's only horrendous if it's true,' Holly responded. 'So is it? Is it true? You only proposed to her because of the accident?'

This wasn't the type of thing good friends did. Backing him into a corner, near enough shouting at him. And she wasn't even sure why she was doing it. But she needed to know the answer. Every part of her needed to know.

'I love Sienna,' Giles said. 'She's smart, she's kind, she's funny, and she's good for me.'

'That doesn't answer the question, though,' Holly said. 'Would you have proposed, had you not had the accident?'

'Maybe not.' He shrugged slightly. 'But maybe that's not a bad thing. That accident gave me the wake-up call I needed. I don't want to be on my own forever, Holly, and I don't need to be. I have an amazing woman who will be a wonderful mother to my children.'

'Jesus, you're talking about children already.'

'Yes, because I'm thinking about the future. It's taken me a long time to get there. To be a person who doesn't just think in the moment. Who acts sensibly, grown-up. That's what you wanted, isn't it? I thought this was the type of person you'd been wanting me to be all along.'

Holly stood there in silence. Everything he had said made perfect sense. And who was to say that one person's reason for proposing wasn't as justified as another's? However he came to the decision, it all boiled down to one point: Giles wanted to spend the rest of his life with Sienna and start a family with her. Why did it matter what had spurred him into popping the question?

Drawing in a deep breath, she unclenched her hands from her sides and slackened the tightness in her jaw.

'Fine,' she said.

'Fine?' Giles raised an eyebrow.

'Fine, I understand. Everything is good.'

His expression didn't change. If anything, it became even more sceptical. 'Really?'

'Yes, I asked a question, and you gave me a reasonable, thought-out answer. That makes perfect sense. Now, if you don't mind, I need to order this fudge. I can't risk the suppliers running out now places are getting busy again.'

Holly lowered her gaze to the laptop, although she could still feel Giles's eyes boring into her. Her mind was too fuzzy. She couldn't even work out how she was meant to open her emails to send an order.

'Do you want me to stay?' he said. 'I don't mind hanging on and giving you a lift back.'

Holly lifted her head and offered him the best smile she could.

'It's fine. It's a nice day, and I've been cramped up behind here for hours. I could do with a proper walk.'

'Right.' Giles's lips parted. For a second, she thought he was going to ask if she wanted company, but he didn't. He just nodded. 'Nothing'll change between us, Holly. You know that, right? We need each other, okay? And I get it's a bit weird at the minute, what with me not telling you before and everything, but we'll be back to normal soon. I promise you.'

'I know,' Holly said, though she could hardly lift her head from her computer to look at him.

'Okay, well, I'll see you in a bit then, I guess.'

A second later, he walked out of the shop, and Holly was left feeling unsure why there was such a hollow pit in her stomach.

20

'This is a good thing,' Holly said to Jamie as she sat at the kitchen island with a glass of wine in her hand. 'Everything he said made perfect sense. And he's right: not every relationship has to be some massive romance. Lots of people get together because it's a convenient, sensible thing to do. Because they've found a steady partnership. I just didn't think that would be something any of us would do, what with you and Fin and—' She stopped. She had been about to say her and Evan, but it didn't feel quite right and so she changed her choice of couple. 'Caroline and Michael. Everyone's always been so in love. But I get it. It makes sense.'

As Holly paused, she looked down at her lap, to where Rhubarb had fallen fast asleep. She was so tiny and so at peace that at times like this, it was almost impossible to remember what a menace she could be. Still, she was her menace, and she wouldn't swap her for the world.

'So, any idea when the wedding is going to be?' Jamie asked, topping up Holly's glass even though it was still half-full. 'Did he mention dates to you yet?'

Holly shook her head. 'No, not yet. Something makes me

think Sienna will need at least a year to plan everything. You know, so she has time to check out a hundred different venues and all that.'

Jamie laughed. 'Well, if it's not gonna be for a while then maybe you've got time to find yourself a plus-one.'

Holly's hand gripped the stem of the glass she was holding tightly. 'Why would I need a plus-one? It's not like I won't know plenty of people there.'

'I know, but it's not about needing a plus-one. It's about wanting one. Like having someone to do that couples dance with after the newlyweds invite you onto the dance floor.'

'Well, I've got Hope for that,' Holly replied curtly. 'And I don't like dancing, anyway.'

'You do after you've had a few drinks,' Jamie said. Her eyes flickered down to her glass before rising to meet Holly's again, and although her gaze was soft, any hint of humour had gone. 'I'm just saying that maybe this would be the right time for you to start thinking about meeting someone. You know, there's this single dad at the playgroup I take the twins to—'

'Stop, stop right now,' Holly said. 'I'm not interested.'

'Well, you might be. He's really, really lovely.'

Holly took a large gulp of her drink. 'If that's the case, then why is he single?'

'Well, from what I gather, it was a bit of a drunken night with his ex that resulted in his son. But they're bringing him up together, like you and Ben. It all seems really amicable. That's got to be a good sign, hasn't it?'

Holly rolled her eyes. She knew there was no point in saying anything, not while Jamie wasn't in the mood to listen. But she wasn't going to be badgered into dating when she wasn't ready. Especially not with some random she'd never even heard of before two minutes ago.

'Maybe when Hope starts secondary school,' she said, hoping the answer would get Jamie off her back. 'When Hope's at secondary school and I've got a bit more time to think, then I'll consider dating.'

Jamie's eyes bugged. 'That's another four years away, Holly.'

'Exactly, so could we stop talking about it and enjoy our evening, please?'

As Holly climbed into bed later that night, she took her phone from her pocket and scrolled through the photos. She'd only bought the phone last year, having held on to her old one for as long as possible because it contained all the photos of her and Evan. Thankfully, Michael had showed her how to transfer them all so they were accessible with whatever device she had. So she could look at them whenever she wanted. Recently, though, she'd been doing so less and less. When she did take five minutes to scan through the images, she tended to look at more recent ones of Hope – Hope doing cartwheels, Hope on the stage. Hope with the other children, causing general mayhem. She couldn't remember the last time she had sat like this, scrolling through one photo after another of her and Evan, trying to recall the memories around the moments.

The longer she looked, the more her heart ached. Every photo was of them smiling or laughing or just being their genuine, silly selves. Even the ones that were just of them in the house, or on a typical, unexciting family walk. He had made the mundane feel special, and she had felt so invincible back then. Like she could achieve anything as long as Evan was by her side. Was that how Giles felt with Sienna? she wondered. It hadn't sounded like that when he had spoken about her. Surely that was what he wanted in a relationship – that was what everybody wanted, didn't they?

With a long sigh, she closed the photos and put her phone on the bedside table. Maybe she needed to stop judging other people's relationships by what she'd had with Evan. Or by what her friends had. Relationships were as individual as the people in them, and she needed to remember that.

As she rolled over, ready to fall asleep, a message came through on her phone. It was probably from Jamie, apologising for the whole dating stuff she had tried to push on her earlier that night and given how Holly wasn't even close to asleep, there didn't seem any point waiting until morning to reply. But as she picked up the phone, she frowned. It wasn't a number she recognised.

Sitting upright in bed, Holly tapped on the screen and opened the message, only to instantly regret it.

> Hi Holly, it's Sienna. Do you think we could get together for a talk?

Her stomach somersaulted. There was no way she was going to be able to sleep now.

21

Holly was sitting up in bed, now wide awake. There was a good chance that there was only one wall between her and Jamie and, if they spoke loud enough, there would be no need for the phone at all, but shouting was a sure way to wake Hope and the other children up. Besides, it wasn't exactly normal behaviour. So a telephone call seemed more appropriate.

Thankfully, Jamie had answered immediately.

'Why do you think she wants to talk to me?' Holly asked.

'She probably wants to talk to you about wedding plans,' she said. 'You are Giles's best woman or whatever he called you. That probably comes with a list of jobs to do. I can imagine Sienna is the type of person who likes lists.'

'I thought that,' Holly agreed. 'But, if that was the case, wouldn't she say, "I want to talk to you about the wedding"? Doesn't the way she worded her message sound a bit creepy? And surely if anyone should have jobs for me to do, it will be Giles, right? She shouldn't be asking me to do things. That's what she has bridesmaids for, surely? Assuming she's having brides-maids. Unless she's not, and that's what she wants to talk to me about. But what if it's not about the wedding at all? What if it's about something different? What would that be? What could she possibly want to talk to me about?'

Holly could feel a panic rising in her chest. None of Giles's girlfriends ever wanted to talk to her. In fact, they normally gave her a peculiarly wide berth. But then Sienna wasn't a girlfriend any more. She was his fiancée.

'I think you're thinking too deeply about this,' Jamie said, causing a momentary halt to Holly's spiralling thoughts. 'It was just a quick text message. And if you're that desperate to find out what she wants, the easiest thing to do would be to message her back.'

Holly had thought the same herself. But then, it was late and Sienna wouldn't be expecting a response at this time. In fact, sending a message this late felt tantamount to disastrous. Had she not been fully awake, Holly could have read the message in a groggy state, then fallen back asleep. She could even have forgotten about the message altogether. Maybe she should pretend that was what she'd done. Opened it half asleep, rolled back in her bed, then forgotten about it. That way, she'd never need to reply and hopefully, Sienna could find someone else to talk to. But then...

'What if it's something bad?' she said, breaking the silence that had formed.

'What could be so terrible?' Jamie said. 'What are you worried about?'

Holly pondered the question for a moment. What was she so worried that Sienna might say?

'I'm not sure,' she said, but the knot in the pit of her stomach confirmed that wasn't true. She knew exactly what she was worried about. She was worried that Sienna was going to tell her it was time that her and Giles's relationship changed. Now that they were engaged, Giles couldn't be her go-to person any more, and she couldn't be his. She was worried Sienna was going to say that she wanted to put some space between them.

That was what was scaring her.

'You know what, you're right. I'm just being ridiculous,' Holly said, brushing the thoughts aside. 'I'll message her back in the morning. I'm sure everything is fine. Sleep well.'

'You too.'

Holly hung up and lay back down on her bed before checking the time on her watch. It was late. Well past the normal time she went to bed. Yet she had a sneaking suspicion she wasn't going to sleep well at all.

22

'Mummy, you already put milk in the bowl. What are you doing? There's already milk. You're going to spill it. And there isn't even any cereal in it yet!'

Holly looked down at the bowl in front of her. Hope was correct. It was currently filled three-quarters full of milk and without a drop of breakfast cereal in there.

'Sorry,' she said, grabbing a mug and pouring off some of the excess. 'Mummy was busy thinking.'

'That doesn't sound good.'

'Hey, you. That's enough of the cheekiness.'

With a roll of her eyes, Hope took the bowl from Holly and finally added cereal to it.

'I didn't say I minded. I like extra milk.'

Holly was definitely distracted, and it was the message from Sienna doing it.

No matter what she'd tried, Holly had found it impossible to sleep with the weight of the unknown bearing down on her. She knew she had to reply. Just send something so she could close her eyes and stop fretting so much. But then what should she say when she didn't know what Sienna wanted to talk about? Agreeing to a meeting when you didn't know the agenda felt like a rookie mistake, yet asking, *Can you tell me what about?* or, *Maybe, but I need to know context first?* just sounded rude.

So it had taken her over twenty-five minutes to settle on a single-word answer of 'sure', and even then she didn't know if that had been the correct thing to write. It didn't help that she still hadn't received a reply.

'Mummy, have you packed my swimming things?' Hope said, bringing Holly out of her constant stream of thoughts. 'You know it's free swim today.'

'Yes, yes, of course,' Holly said.

'And have you fed Rhubarb today, because she's drinking the milk out of your mug?'

'Get out of there,' Holly said, grabbing the kitten and putting her back down on the floor next to her biscuits. As soon as the cat started eating, Holly headed back to the worktop and picked up her phone again.

A pang of self-annoyance struck. She needed to get over this. Whatever it was, she couldn't lose her entire day worrying about it and yet as she was debating whether she should ring Giles, just to find out what was going on, her phone buzzed again and a message flashed up on the screen. Without thinking, she swiped to open it.

> Great! Why don't I come to yours tonight around seven? I'll bring the wine.

Holly swallowed. Why had she opened the message straight away? Sienna was probably still holding her phone, which meant she could see Holly was online. That meant Holly had to either reply or have it be very obvious that she was ignoring her.

Not able to bring herself to write any words, she sent a

smiley-face emoji back. A smiley face, nothing more, and yet its meaning was perfectly clear. She and Sienna were going to talk.

23

The morning went from bad to worse. Before Holly had even unlocked the front door of the shop, Greta rang in sick. Frustratingly, Caroline was off in London for the day doing a university visit with Tim and even her father was busy taking part in his first ever lawn bowls tournament, which meant Holly was on her own. From the moment she saw the clouds clear to reveal a bright-blue sky and the first bus-full of tourists roll into the village, she knew it was going to be busy and she wasn't wrong. Normally, busy was great. Busy was what kept her business running. But busy when it was also boiling hot and there was no chance of escape, even for a lunch break, was pretty unbearable.

Even though the shop had air conditioning, it was directed over the chocolate, because, no matter how disgusting she felt, Holly was allowed to melt. The chocolate wasn't. To make matters worse, because of the cloud cover when she'd left the house, she had worn a long-sleeved shirt and jeans, which by lunchtime were feeling less than pristine. All she wanted to do was switch the door sign to *Closed* and enjoy all the tourists paddling in the river, but there was no chance of that happening.

Her only minute of respite came when Jamie brought her a top and she got to dash upstairs and change, before the twins caused too much destruction.

The second she turned the sign to *Closed*, Holly was done. Hope was staying the night at Ben's, and all Holly wanted was to have a very long shower, then lie down on the sofa and watch a film. But that wasn't going to happen. Sienna had already reconfirmed that she would be there at seven, not only with wine but with nibbles too.

> You don't have to; I have plenty.

Holly had sent her reply, already suspecting Sienna would not be deterred. She was right. When she showed up at Holly's door, exactly at seven thirty, she was weighed down with bags.

'I got a bit carried away,' she said, taking one item after another out of the canvas totes and placing them on the counter. 'But I realised I didn't know what you liked. It's ridiculous, isn't it? You're my fiancé's best friend, and I don't even know what type of olives you like.'

'I'm not actually a great olive fan,' Holly admitted. 'Unless it's in bread or tapenade.'

'I should've got tapenade!' Sienna said, her face distraught.

'Really, we have plenty of food here. This was very generous of you,' Holly said. 'What do you want to drink? I've got some wine already chilled.'

'Whatever you have is fine, honestly. That'll be absolutely great. As long as it's British or French, that is.'

'Right, yes.' Holly went to the fridge and pulled out a half-full bottle of Marlborough Sauvignon Blanc. 'It's Australian,' she said, not sure why she suddenly felt so guilty about the origin of her wine. 'We'll open one of yours.'

'No, no, it's fine, honestly. Some of the Australian wines are lovely. And it does one good to stretch one's palate, doesn't it?'

'Okay.'

Holly pulled out two glasses and took her time pouring their drinks. Any doubt she'd had that this evening might not be as awkward as she'd feared was rapidly evaporating. If not having tapenade and buying wine from the wrong country was what Sienna found issues with, Holly couldn't imagine what they were going to talk about.

'There you go,' Holly said, as she gave Sienna the drink, although she didn't immediately take a sip.

'It's about the carbon footprint,' she said.

'Sorry?'

'I just feel terrible about drinking things that have been shipped all the way from the other side of the world, you know, when there are things that are made closer to home. I know that France isn't close, but you know, it's not that I'm being a snob about the wine.'

'Oh right, no, I didn't think that you were,' Holly lied.

'Yes, you did.'

'Yes, you're right, I did.'

The pair let out a brief chuckle that ended as Holly took her first sip of the drink. She had to admit carbon footprints were something she never thought about, but maybe that was a major flaw on her part. After all, she wanted to leave the planet in the best possible state for Hope and any possible grandchildren.

As the two women sipped, Holly became aware of the tension weaving its way into the silence. At some point, one of them was going to have to speak. Either that or they would end up downing their entire glasses without exchanging a single word. As hard as she tried to think, though, she couldn't figure out what to say, and why should she be the one to start the conversation, anyway?

Sienna was the one who wanted to talk. That was her specific reason for coming over. But with every passing second, the silence was becoming more and more obvious and as she took yet another mouthful of her wine, Holly couldn't bear it any longer.

'So what did you—'

'Thank you for—'

The pair spoke simultaneously.

'Sorry,' Holly said. 'You speak first.'

'I was just saying thank you for having me round like this.'

'You're welcome.'

'I know this isn't something you and I have done before, but I'd like it if maybe we could do it more often.'

'Maybe,' Holly said, only to realise how lame her answer sounded. 'That would be nice.'

Sienna laughed. It was far more genuine and chestier than the earlier chuckle she had offered.

'You're a terrible liar,' she said. 'But I mean it. I know it's strange for us, this relationship, but I think it would make Giles really happy if you and I could be friends. Proper friends, you know.'

'Yes, I'm sure you're right.'

'He thinks the absolute world of you, and Hope too. I mean, you're practically family.'

Holly's throat tightened as her pulse picked up. She wasn't sure why Sienna was suddenly making her feel so nervous, but the tension she'd assumed would fade when they started talking was now worse. 'You know what our friendship group is like,' she said. 'We're all very close.'

'Yes,' Sienna said. 'But it's different with you and him. He was in love with you for a long time, right?'

24

Holly was sure she was being set up. This had to be some kind of trap, right? How the hell was she supposed to give an answer that Sienna would actually want to hear?

'Did Giles tell you that?' she asked, eventually.

It was Sienna's turn to take an unusually long sip of wine.

'Sort of. Not directly. He said there was someone he had been in love with for a very long time. Someone who couldn't be with him. He said that it had been difficult to fully open up his heart again after she rejected him. Repeatedly. That's you he's talking about, isn't it? You're the one who didn't want to be with Giles, even though he was in love with you?'

'It wasn't quite that simple.' Holly felt like she was being attacked. The way Sienna had said the word 'repeatedly', like it had been dozens of times and it wasn't anything like that at all. She could count on one hand the number of times she and Giles had really spoken about their feelings for one another. 'There was a lot going on in my life. Having Hope with Ben, and there was Evan and—'

'Holly, I'm not judging you. Really, I'm not, and I hope it

doesn't come across that way. I just wanted you to know that I understand now that this is probably difficult for you. I think for a long time you've been his number one and now that's going to change.'

'Well...' Holly began, not sure how she was going to continue, but as it happened, she didn't get a chance.

'It has to change. You understand that, right?' Sienna carried on. 'And if there is a chance that you do have feelings for Giles... if this proposal has suddenly made you feel like you were wrong in rejecting him and you're going to come after him, I need to know that now. I don't want to be anybody's pity prize, but I'm not letting you ruin what we have, just because you think you have some sort of entitlement—'

'What?' Holly's tongue lolled uselessly in her mouth. 'I don't feel like that at all. Giles and I... We're... We're... Giles is just a friend. A really good friend, but that's it. That's all we've ever been. All we ever will be.'

Sienna's relief was palpable. 'You have no idea how relieved I am to hear you say that. Honestly, because I really like you, Holly. I want to get to know you properly. You probably think it's silly, but I was so worried about having this conversation. I must have written at least a dozen messages trying to make sure I got the tone right.'

'That doesn't sound silly. Not at all,' Holly replied.

'Thank you. So... with that out the way, I should tell you the other reason I wanted to talk.'

'There's another reason?' Holly tried not to show her horror, yet she obviously didn't do a great job, as Sienna let out a little chuckle.

'There's a wonderful little spa hotel up in Norfolk. Very exclusive. In fact, I had to book the rooms two years ago just to get in, and I had no idea who I was going to take. I just didn't want to miss out on the chance, you understand?'

'I think—'

'Well, the booking is for two weeks' time and it's definitely not Giles's type of place. So I thought that maybe you and Faye could come instead. You were saying at the hospital how you hadn't had a chance to catch up properly in ages, and Giles said she's not had a proper break since the children were born and I thought it could be a really great chance for us all to bond? What do you say? Please say yes. It'll be just perfect. I know it will.'

Holly knew what she wanted to say. What single-syllable word was teetering on the end of her tongue. But she couldn't do it. Not with Sienna looking up at her wide-eyed and hopeful. Like it or not, she knew there was only one answer she could give and so she smiled as high as her cheeks would allow, wondering if Sienna could feel how fake it felt.

'Sure,' she said. 'That sounds great.'

25

'It sounds terrible,' Holly said to Jamie as they sat in the garden, watching the children make a den for woodlice out of leaves and twigs and anything else they could find. It had been almost a fortnight since Sienna had suggested they go away for a weekend with Faye, and since then, it had been all guns blazing. A group chat had been set up, in which Sienna informed them she had not only booked the rooms, but the train, and even a taxi back from the station to the hotel. She was also bringing a selection of books that they would be welcome to borrow, unless they wanted to buddy read, in which case they would need to get their own copies to join in. According to her, there was nothing for the others to do but enjoy themselves and this was the part Holly was finding the hardest to accept.

'I thought Ben could be controlling, but she's on a whole different level. My only option is to be sick. I could say I had food poisoning, right? That'd be believable. She's got to have another friend who can take my place. Someone who actually likes her.'

Jamie's withering glare said a lot, but mostly how much of a cow Holly was being. And she knew it was true.

'I thought you wanted to get to know her better,' Jamie said. 'Why did you agree otherwise?'

'What else was I meant to say? She had brought wine and nibbles and I felt cornered.'

'Well, that will teach you to grow more of a spine.'

Holly and Jamie had become so close over the years, they were more like siblings than friends, but just like with siblings, it meant that Holly was struck with the occasional urge to thump her and right now was one of those moments.

'You still haven't told me what you spent the rest of the evening talking about,' Jamie said, moving the conversation away from helping Holly get out of the weekend. 'She was over for quite a while.'

'How do you know how long she stayed?'

'I saw her car when I was leaving.'

'You were spying on me?'

'I was not spying on you. We share a driveway, remember? And you're being evasive. What was it about?'

Holly drew in a long breath. She had avoided mentioning the other purpose of Sienna's visit to Jamie and had managed to go two weeks without divulging the contents of their initial conversation to her or anyone else. But now that a chunk of time had passed, it felt silly not to say anything.

'She wanted to know if I had any feelings for Giles. She knew he'd been in love with me before.'

Jamie's lips twisted in a manner Holly couldn't quite read. 'She knew Giles loved you?'

'And she wanted to check there weren't any residual unrequited feelings. On my part, obviously.'

'And what did you tell her?'

'What do you think I told her?' For the second time in as many minutes, Holly was struck with the same urge to thump her friend on the shoulder. 'No. I told her no. What else would I say?'

Jamie didn't respond. Instead, she nodded slowly.

'What? What is it?' The churning in Holly's stomach told her that the next words to leave Jamie's lips were unlikely to lighten her mood.

'I was just thinking about Sienna,' Jamie replied. 'It must've taken a lot of guts to do that. I'm not sure I could ever have confronted Fin's exes.'

'Well, first off, you live in a different country to them, and second, Giles is not my ex. He's just my friend.'

'So you keep telling yourself.'

Holly had had enough. The innuendos had been getting stronger and stronger ever since Giles and Sienna's engagement was announced.

'If there's something you want to say, why don't you come out and say it?' she challenged.

'Fine,' Jamie said, putting her wine down on the table with such force, it splattered. 'You want to know the truth? Here it is: you've never truly let yourself think about whether you and Giles might be good as more than friends. And you would be. We can all see it. What you share isn't platonic, Holly. Not on your part and certainly not on Giles's. It never has been. A man doesn't ask his best girl friend to pick him up from the hospital when he has an actual girlfriend who would be there in an instant. And you wouldn't have dropped everything and raced over there unless your feelings were seriously deep. And I'm worried that by the time you finally realise what you actually feel, it might be too late to do anything about it.'

For a split second, Holly didn't know what to say. Was that really what everyone thought? Were they just waiting for her and Giles to finally get together? No.

Holly let out a long breath. 'Giles and I are best as friends.'

Still, Jamie's gaze was unwavering. 'As long as you're sure about that.'

'I am,' Holly said with all the firmness she could muster. 'I absolutely am.'

'Well, in that case, this weekend away could be a lot of fun. You know what, I'll even help you pack.'

26

As much as Holly hoped the next forty-eight hours would bring about a sudden, overnight tummy bug, or at the very least, a decent head cold, she was truly disappointed to remain in perfect health, and Friday afternoon as she kissed Hope goodbye and headed to the railway station, she knew exactly what awaited her: a relaxing weekend of reading and catching up with Faye, and trying to get to know Sienna better too. Jamie's words had irked her so much, she had thought about little else. Suggesting she could have feelings for Giles was a ridiculous thing to say, and she was going to prove it. She was going to learn all she could about Sienna, and who knew, by the end of the weekend, they might actually be friends.

'You have no idea how much I need this weekend,' Faye said as the train drew away from the platform. 'You know, the longest stint Gavin's ever done on his own with the kids is one evening, and I had to put them to bed before I went out. Seriously, he's not going to know what's hit him. And he's under strict instructions not to call me. At all.'

Holly felt a pang of gratitude towards Ben. They had always

split the parenting fifty-fifty. In fact, when Hope had been little, everything had come so naturally to him, she'd found it hard not to feel like the inferior parent. And even now, with two more girls at home, Hope couldn't have wished for a more attentive or loving father. Of course, Ben wasn't the only great dad out there. She knew that.

'I suspect Giles will want to be far more full-on when you have children,' Faye said, her line of thought obviously similar to Holly's.

'Oh, we won't be having children,' Sienna said.

Holly's chest involuntarily spasmed as she looked at Faye. She saw she'd had a similar reaction.

'I'm so sorry,' Faye started. 'I shouldn't have—'

'No, it's fine,' Sienna said. 'I mean, I can have children. I assume. But I've never wanted any. They just take over your life, don't they?'

'Yes,' Holly said, still struggling to find her voice. 'That's kind of the point of having them.'

'Exactly. I completely get it. You have a child, you have to make them your priority, and I don't want to do that. I've spent my entire adult life learning to make myself a priority. And it's finally got me somewhere in life where I'm happy. Why would I risk upsetting that?'

Holly hoped it was a rhetorical question, because she couldn't think of a reply. She would never judge anyone for not wanting children. Each person's life was their own, to live exactly as they wanted to, and Sienna's response made sense. Only this wasn't just Sienna's life she was talking about. It was Giles's too.

'And is Giles okay with that?' Faye said, voicing the thought in Holly's head.

Sienna shrugged. 'He'll come around to my way of thinking. I'm very persuasive.' She let out a little giggle, but Holly couldn't reciprocate and from the way the colour had drained from Faye's face, neither could she. Silence threatened to form, and Holly knew she had to say something. Like how marrying someone with a very different vision for the future wasn't a great idea. After all, Giles had said to her plain as day that he wanted children before he got old. That was part of his reason for proposing.

Surely Sienna knew that? She cleared her throat, still not sure how she was going to word her statement, when Faye suddenly sparked into life.

'I almost forgot. I brought us a couple of goodies to get the weekend started.' She reached into her bag and pulled out three miniature bottles of Prosecco. As she handed Holly hers, she met her eyes, offering a look that said now wasn't the time to cause issues. Holly got it. Fingers crossed there would be another opportunity, later on in the weekend, to voice her opinion on the matter.

'The breakfast buffet, that is what I am looking forward to,' Faye said as she went back to her bag to retrieve plastic cups. 'Getting up late, rolling out of bed to every kind of pastry and savoury that I can eat, then rolling to the poolside. There is a pool at this place, right?'

'Oh yes, there is. I can't wait for you to see it. Now, let's get a selfie. I've promised Giles I'd do lots of check-ins to tell him how everything is going.'

Before Holly could even put her drink down, Sienna had lifted her phone and angled it towards them. Yet rather than looking at the screen, to ensure she wasn't pulling some hideous face, Holly was distracted by the ring on Sienna's finger.

Holly remembered with acute detail how Caroline had forced her to look at the ring during the engagement. She recalled the way the light had glinted off it, and how Sienna had described it as delicate and understated, yet in a manner that didn't make those sound like positive attributes. But this ring was anything but understated. The diamond was colossal, and even the band was studded with more smaller stones. Had the band had diamonds in before? No, she would have remembered that, wouldn't she?

Unable to let the issue go, she turned away from the camera to look directly at Sienna.

'Did you get a new engagement ring?' she asked.

27

As the question continued to buzz around in Holly's mind, Sienna placed her phone down on the table and lifted her hand up. The manner in which she twisted her wrist from side to side was almost identical to how she had done after her engagement, but there was no doubt that this was a different ring on her finger to the one Holly had been made to admire before.

'Isn't this one stunning?' she said, her eyes glimmering almost as much as the diamond.

'I don't understand. What about the one Giles proposed with?'

Sienna rolled her eyes slightly.

'It was very sweet and everything. And the sentiment was there, obviously. I'm so glad he got a diamond ring to propose properly with, but it was hardly the type of thing you want to show people when you tell them you've got engaged, was it? I mean, it was only just a carat. It didn't feel right, having something so little. An engagement ring's meant to be a statement, you know? A sign of what your married life is going to be like. And this one, this one makes a much bigger statement, don't you think? Honestly, given our positions in life, you know, our age and how well we're both doing, I think the jeweller really should have insisted that he look at nothing below the two-carat mark. But I've rectified that now. This one's perfect. A two-point-five-carat centre, with an extra carat in the halo and pavé. All conflict-free, obviously. That was an absolute must.'

Holly stared again at the ring and then glanced down at the one on her finger. In terms of size, it was far bigger than she'd ever envisioned herself wearing, but what size carat it was, and whether or not it was conflict-free, she had no idea. She'd not had the chance to ask Evan that.

Swallowing down a lump that was forming in her throat, she looked back at Sienna's hand. It was a stunning ring. Excessive, possibly, but beautiful. And if Giles had the money to spend on a ring like that, then why shouldn't he? Why shouldn't Sienna have the piece of jewellery she wanted if it was what she was going to be wearing for the rest of her life? Who was Holly to judge that?

And yet, if Evan had proposed to her with a piece of string, she would've kept that tied on her finger for all eternity, because in her mind, it wasn't the ring that was a sign of what your married life was going to be like; it was the thought that went behind it. Surely?

'Well, while we're on the conversation of rings, it feels like a good time to start wedding talk,' Sienna said, placing one hand down on the table in front of her as she took a minuscule sip of her Prosecco. 'I thought we could start by talking about colour schemes. I want something that won't date, but still doesn't look dated. So come on, fire ideas at me. I'm ready to hear anything.'

28

People were multifaceted, Holly got that. She had several sides to her. The people at the sweet shop only ever got to see the happy, smiling Holly, but there was also the grumpy version of her that sat at her computer for hours doing her tax refunds, the Holly who volunteered reading with the children at Hope's school, and the one who more than once considered whether she should sell the sweet shop and train to become a primary school teacher. There was the Holly who liked nothing more than quiet evenings by herself, but also the one who liked joking and whiling away the hours, drinking wine with her friends. All people were multifaceted; she understood that. But with Sienna, it was like the woman had so many strands and viewpoints, it was impossible to keep track of them all. Let alone get an idea of who she actually was as a person.

'I know these charity events aren't about how you look,' she said. They were over an hour into the train journey, and they had already moved on from the conversation about wedding clothes to clothes in general. 'But it matters. It really does. It's hard to make someone donate large quantities of hard-earned money to your cause if you're dressed in a manner that stops them from speaking to you in the first place. You need to attract their attention. Then, once you've got them in, once they think they know the type of person you are, that's when you turn things around and then start with the heavy-hitting stuff. But I wouldn't be able to get to that point if they didn't take notice of me first. Designer gear helps with that. And as an added bonus, it means I get to spend lots of money on gorgeous clothes and accessories. If people assume I'm shallow because of that, then that's up to them.'

It was a fair enough point, Holly considered, although she couldn't deny that was what she'd done: met Sienna and judged her as the type of person she wouldn't want to be friends with. So what did that say about Giles? The fact he proposed to her probably meant he had stuck around long enough to find out more. And yet the thing with the ring still left a bad taste at the back of her mouth, not to mention her comment about not wanting children, even though she knew Giles did. Still, Holly had a full weekend to get through. If she didn't keep an open mind about Sienna, it was going to be an incredibly long forty-eight hours. At some point, she would definitely need to get Faye's opinion on the situation.

'I've already arranged a taxi to pick us up from the station,' Sienna said as their stop approached. 'It's just a fourteen-minute drive, traffic dependent, and I don't want to spoil anything, but this place is so special. You're going to love it. I'm absolutely positive you're going to love it.'

'Buffet and pool,' Faye repeated. 'Oh, and a comfy bed. Those are my three requirements.'

'Well, you'll definitely get two out of three of those,' Sienna replied.

Two out of three, Holly thought. It felt like a peculiar thing to say, and she was about to ask Sienna what she meant when the train tannoy announced their station.

'Make sure you've got everything, girls,' Sienna said. 'If you forget your swimsuit, then you'll be stuck. I doubt you'll be able to fit into one of mine. At the minute anyway. Fingers crossed this weekend will help.'

29

Holly couldn't move. She had misheard, surely? She had to have misheard. Sienna couldn't possibly have commented on her and Faye's weight, could she? Who in their right mind would do that? Holly looked to Faye, hoping she could get some confirmation that she wasn't going insane, but Faye's head was under the train table, trying to find something she'd obviously dropped.

'Here, let me grab that for you,' Sienna said, bending to the floor and reaching out to pick up whatever it was Faye had dropped. A moment later, she was up again and placing a keyring on the table while Faye was still struggling to get out of the gap and stand upright. 'The doors are opening. Don't worry, I'll go hold them. You two just make sure we haven't forgotten anything.'

With that, she darted off to hold the train doors open while Faye gathered her items. Holly remained standing in the aisle, still unable to move.

'Did you hear what she just said?' she asked, keeping her voice low so as not to be overheard by Sienna. Not that it was

likely. She was already miles away, and there were plenty of
people between them.

'What? About keeping the doors open?' Faye asked. 'Thank
goodness. Still, we'd better hurry. Sorry about that. I tell Gavin off
for always dropping things, but sometimes I'm just as bad.'

'No, it's not... I meant... Never mind,' Holly said. 'I'm sure it
was nothing.'

A few minutes later, they were in the taxi driving up towards
the venue, and Holly was trying to push the thought from her
mind. The train had been braking, and other people were
standing up to get their bags too. There was a good chance she'd
completely misheard. Although what Sienna could have possibly
said that sounded so similar, Holly wasn't sure.

You actually have to make an effort, you know, Holly heard
Jamie's voice ringing in her ears, that and the comment about
never liking any of Giles's girlfriends, never giving them a chance.
That wouldn't be the case this time. She was going to get to know
Sienna properly. At least that way, she'd know any judgements
she made were fair and would have hard evidence to come back
to Jamie with.

'Look, deer!' Faye said, pointing out the window.

'Lots of deer.' Sure enough, a small herd was grazing in the
fields.

'It's stunning, isn't it?' Sienna said. 'Just stunning.'

'It really is,' Holly replied. Much to her surprise, she could
feel a slight heat building in her eyes. Growing up, she had never
imagined this type of life for herself. Security – that was where
her dreams ended: marriage, a house, children, and a steady job
that meant the bills were paid when they came through each
month. Never had she dreamt of a life like the one she had: a
successful business owner, with a new possibility of travelling
abroad for work – if this thing with Fin's friend worked out.

With a jolt of guilt, Holly realised she still hadn't got his number from Fin. Somehow, the engagement had knocked everything else out of kilter in her life and she couldn't even remember important things like that. But this evening, she would get on top of it. Still, she couldn't complain about life. She had a friendship group she would put her life on the line for and moments like this, where she was whisked away to an enchanting corner of the country ready for a weekend of luxury. A weekend Sienna had arranged for them. She would bear that in mind the next time she thought she heard her say something mean. Mean people didn't do such nice things, did they?

'Thank you,' she said, needing to voice the moment. 'Thank you for arranging all this. It's lovely.'

Sienna beamed. 'Oh, I'm so glad you like it. I know this type of thing can be a bit unique. It's not everyone's cup of tea, but I just knew that you were the type of girls who would be on board with it. And everyone loves a weekend when you leave looking even better than you arrived, right? That's what every bride-to-be needs.'

Holly's feeling of elation stuttered slightly as she cast a glance at Faye, who shrugged, clearly as confused about the statement as Holly. Was it a subtle dig about her weight again? Sure, Holly had put on a few pounds over the last couple of years, but she had needed to after all the weight she'd lost after Evan's death. This time, she was going to get some clarification as to what the hell Sienna meant, yet as she opened her mouth, Faye let out a squeal.

'Are you serious? That is amazing!'

'Isn't it phenomenal?' Sienna said.

'Wow. Oh my God. I've never seen anything like it.'

Distracted by the sudden exclamations, Holly turned her attention out the window. The air hitched in her lungs. She was used to beautiful buildings. There was no shortage of them in the Cotswolds. No shortage even in Bourton itself. But this wasn't like the buildings she was used to. This wasn't made of Cotswold stone, or beautiful red bricks, or any stone at all that Holly could tell – not on the outside, at least. The outside of the building was made from dark timber. But it was the angle at which it was arranged that was most mesmerising. The wood flowed out and in, in an almost concertina-like manner or ripples, caused by a pebble in a still pond. Lead tinted glass windows, also at similarly curved angles, broke up the mass of wood, and as Holly stared at the feat of architecture, she could help but think that the shape reminded her of something. Though what that was, she couldn't quite work out. Not until Faye spoke.

'Looks like a spaceship,' she said.

'That's what it is,' Holly said. 'Yes, you're right. It's like a wooden glass spaceship.'

'It's an incredible building,' Sienna said. 'Apparently, the inside is even more extravagant than the outside. But I couldn't find any pictures of it online. They are so exclusive, they don't share things like that and you have to sign a document saying you won't share images on social media. I can't wait to see it, though.'

The building was a far cry from the stereotypical English manor you'd expect a spa weekend to be held in, but as long as the pool was clean and the food was good, Holly wasn't going to mind at all. In fact, for the first time since she had accepted the invitation, she was actually starting to feel excited. Very excited.

30

Three minutes later, they were standing in the hotel foyer. Sienna was right; it was extraordinary. The desks were all made of hammered copper, while the chairs, which looked comfy enough, were made of plastic that had been shaped to look as though the legs were melting into the floor. The lighting came from a long pillar placed in the centre of the room, which also acted as a water feature. And though Holly wasn't able to name the aroma that rose in clouded plumes from various diffusers, luxury was the word that sprang to mind whenever she inhaled.

'Welcome to You-Topia.' The lady at the desk drew Holly's attention momentarily away from the decor and smells. Holly couldn't help but give an involuntary shudder at the woman's attire, which was pristine white from head to toe. If she'd had to wear something like that for work, Holly doubted it would last more than ten minutes without her spilling something down it. She and white did not mix well.

'Miss Sommercroft, I assume?' the woman said.

Sienna bounded towards her. 'Yes, that's us. Thank you so much. We are so excited. I've wanted to come here for years.'

'Yes, well, we're very pleased to meet you and I hope we surpass all your expectations.'

'I'm sure you will.'

She was almost as excited at this hotel as she had been about Giles's proposal, Holly thought, but she quickly quashed the thought. Of course she was excited. Anyone who booked a place with a two-year waiting list was bound to be excited about it.

'I'll get a member of staff to show you to your room shortly,' the lady said. 'But before you go, I would just like to get your dinner order. You will be eating in tonight, I assume?'

'Of course,' Sienna replied.

'Wonderful. Well, if you'd like to take a look at the menu...' The woman handed a small piece of laminated cardboard to Sienna, at which point, Holly and Faye both stepped forward to take theirs.

Holly was used to small menus. Her time with Evan had seen her visit a remarkable number of restaurants that served very limited choices, including a Brazilian place that only served three dishes a day. At the other end of the scale, they also ate at one restaurant with a twenty-course degustation meal. But this menu was even more unusual.

The first item was entitled *Invigoration* and apparently involved a number of fruits and vegetables that no one would ever put together to form a meal: guava, celery, dragon fruit, grass, and pomelo. Holly wasn't in the mood for some bizarre salad, so she let her eyes move on to the next item. This one was entitled *Revitalise*. Again, it came with a mix of fruit and vegetables, including rambutan and red cabbage.

Holly found she was missing something somewhere. Perhaps she just had the drinks menu, rather than the food one. Yes, that was the most likely thing – all the strangely named fruits and vegetables were obviously in smoothies.

'Sorry,' she said to the receptionist. 'I think I've been given the drinks menu?'

'Yes?'

'Well, I was hoping I could see the actual menu,' Holly said, not sure why the issue needed explaining further.

'That is our dinner menu,' she said. 'You will get a different one for lunch and breakfast.'

Holly pressed her thumb into her temple, not sure why this simple request was proving so difficult.

'No, sorry, I meant the food menu.'

'Food?' Sienna had now joined in the conversation too, although she was currently looking at Holly with an expression of pure perplexity.

'Yes, food,' Holly said. 'Like burgers or salads or pizza, that type of thing.'

At this, the woman threw back her head and laughed. 'Oh, look at you. Aren't you funny? You almost had me there.'

Holly looked at Faye, who was holding the same menu and also looking somewhat confused, but it was Sienna who stood up and rested a hand on Holly's shoulder.

'Sorry, I should've explained,' she said. 'It's a raw-food, juice-only detoxing spa. Fantastic, isn't it?'

31

Holly was waiting for the moment. The moment when Sienna threw back her head and laughed in a remarkably similar manner to that of the receptionist. Or maybe she would slap Holly on the back and say, 'Gotcha,' or something equally cheesy. The moment was definitely going to come, wasn't it?

Holly blinked a couple of times, opened her mouth, but found no words came out.

'Wow, a juice spa. That is definitely something I'd never thought about doing.' Faye broke the silence as she walked towards them. 'But I'm sure it'll be loads of fun, don't you think, Holly? Holly?'

Even though her name was spoken, Holly took a moment to respond.

'What? Oh, yes, right. Absolutely. Right... juice for lunch. And dinner?'

'For three meals a day,' the woman countered. 'Plus, we do a mid-morning and mid-afternoon shot.'

'Of alcohol?' Holly asked hopefully.

'Of detoxifying probiotics,' the woman replied.

'Right,' Holly said.

'I can put you all down for the daily specials if you would like? They are our most popular choice.'

'That sounds perfect,' Sienna said. 'Right girls? Three daily specials?'

'That sounds great,' Faye replied, while Holly choked out a noise that sounded somewhere between a grunt and a sneeze, that everyone took as agreement.

With their meals written down, the receptionist smiled broadly.

'Now, let's show you up to your rooms. Dominique, can you get the ladies' bags please?'

After Dominique, the bellboy, appeared from some hidden corner of the foyer and stacked their bags onto a thin trolley, Holly walked in silence at the back of the group. Juice, for an entire weekend. It wasn't like she was a sugar addict or anything. Or no more addicted than the average person, anyway. Given how she spent most of her waking hours in a sweet shop, she had to make a conscious effort to ensure that she wasn't constantly tucking into the sherbet lemons and chocolate-covered Brazil nuts. But a couple of small treats a day were expected in a role like hers.

Naturally, her love of baking also meant she was partial to the odd sweet treat there too, and normally she had a cake or biscuit for dessert. There was definitely sugar in those; she measured it out herself. But she still wouldn't consider it an addiction. The same way she wouldn't consider the glass of wine she had with Jamie most evenings an alcohol addiction. But then wine had sugar in too, didn't it? Crap, who was she kidding? Two full days of just juice? How the hell was she going to cope with that?

She was about to ask if there were any other alternative options, on the possibility that she simply couldn't survive on a mixture of cashew nut milk, açai, dragon fruit, and whatever other strange concoctions were in the specialist juices. But before she could speak, she heard a gasp.

'Oh my God, it's absolutely stunning!' It was Faye's voice, although almost immediately followed by Sienna's.

'Wow, I mean, I knew it was special, but wow, this is incredible!'

Momentarily pushing thoughts of food to the back of her mind, Holly stepped forward and looked into the room.

'Wow,' she said.

There were two double beds, all made with perfectly white linen, a bright contrast to the incredible dark wood of the walls. The paintings – they were all paintings, not prints or reproductions – were vibrant and yet tasteful and the walls had been painted with an ombré effect that ended at exactly the same shade of navy blue as the carpet, giving a feeling of continuity that was almost dizzying. But the star of the show was definitely the windows. The angle at which they had been installed flooded the room with light. But it was more than that. It made it feel as if the room was outside, as if they were at one with nature. It was absolutely breathtaking.

'Sienna, this is beautiful,' she said.

Sienna turned around and beamed.

'Well, we have two rooms. Dominique tells me the one next door is just a single double. It's up to you; I don't mind sharing with one you girls or—'

'No, no, it's absolutely fine,' Holly said. 'You take the room to yourself. We'll share this one. You're all right with that, aren't you, Faye?'

It took Holly a moment to register Faye's response, due to it being muffled by cushions.

'I am never getting off this bed,' she said, as she lay spread-eagled on the double bed, having appeared to have sunk a good two inches into the duvet.

Maybe juices wouldn't be that bad, Holly conceded. After all, they could have a nice early night, make the most of the comfy beds, perhaps put a film on for the three of them. And there was still the spa and pool. Although she would have to make sure she didn't spend too much time swimming. Swimming always made her hungry, and on a weekend like this, that would be less than ideal.

'So, why don't we all get changed and head downstairs? We can have a dip before dinner. I can't wait for you to see the pool,' Sienna said. 'I know you guys are just going to love it.'

Holly was about to reply when she felt her phone buzz in her pocket.

'Sure, sounds good,' she said hastily, retrieving it. She assumed it would be Ben or Jamie or someone checking in on her, but instead, it was from Giles, and rather than a text message, he was ringing her.

'Everything okay?' Sienna said.

Holly went to respond, only to hesitate.

'Yes, I just... I'm just gonna head outside to take this.'

'No problem.'

The moment Holly was out of the door, she began running down the corridor. She wasn't sure why she wanted to be as far away from Sienna as possible before she picked up the phone, but she did.

32

'Hey, what's going on? Why are you ringing me? Is everything okay?' Holly carried on walking as she spoke.

'Wow, that's a lot of panic. Most people just answer the phone with "hello".'

Holly gritted her teeth. Of course, Giles wasn't going to respond sensibly.

'Hello. Now, why are you ringing me? Is everything okay?'

'Everything is great on this end; I just wanted to check on you guys. Have you got there yet? Sienna was so excited about the place.'

'Well, it's certainly unique.'

A pause followed. Normally, she could read Giles's pauses down the telephone line just as well as she could read them on his face, but she was having difficulty. Probably because she didn't know why he'd rung her.

'I still don't know why you're ringing?' she said. 'I thought Sienna was keeping you updated on our progress? You know, with the selfies and stuff.' Thinking of the photo Sienna took on the train jolted Holly's memory of the ring. She wanted to talk to

Giles about it, at some point, but it didn't feel like the right time. Particularly as he was struggling to make any sense.

'She is…' he says. 'No, it's fine, I just—'

'You just what?' Holly said. 'Spit it out, will you?'

'Okay, I just wanted to ask you to be nice.'

'What? Are you kidding? Be nice? What's that supposed to mean? I am nice!'

'I know you're nice; you are a lovely, wonderful person. I just need you to be nice to Sienna because—'

'Because she's the type of person who would make you trade the perfectly beautiful and thoughtful engagement ring you had bought her for something bigger and more expensive because she needed it to make a statement?'

So much for not saying anything.

'Ahh, yeah, so she told you about that.'

'No, she didn't. I spotted it wasn't the same and asked her about it.'

'It's her prerogative, you know. It is her ring. The last thing I'd want is for her to be unhappy. And by the way, this is why I was ringing to ask you to be nice. Because I knew you'd judge her for that.'

'Who says I'm judging her?'

'You're judging, Holly. I can tell you are.'

She bit on the inside of her cheek. Now that the ring had been mentioned, she could probably bring up the children issue too, but that felt like something that needed to be done in person.

'Have you told Faye this as well?' she said instead as she continued her stroll. There didn't seem any harm in having a little exploration while they were talking. 'Have you rung her, or are you going to ring her? Does she need telling to be nice?'

'No, don't be daft, because Faye's… she's my sister; she doesn't have a choice in this. It matters, okay? This weekend, it matters a lot to Sienna, and therefore, it matters to me, and if it matters to me, I know it will also matter to you.'

'Is that right?'

'I'm serious, Hol. I need you and her to get on well. I'm not sure what I'd do if you didn't.'

'Well, you'd have to find a new friendship group,' Holly said jokingly, only for a loud sigh to reverberate down the line. One that she reciprocated almost immediately. 'Giles, I know. I was just being silly. I'll be nice.'

'Promise?'

'Promise.'

'Great, that's all I rang for. I shall let you get to your relaxing.'

'Thank you.'

She was about to end the call when she remembered something. 'By the way, did you know – did you know this place is a—?'

But it was already too late; he'd hung up on her.

33

It was only now she'd stopped walking that Holly realised how far she had gone during her little chat with Giles. She was all the way downstairs again, but rather than heading towards the foyer, she seemed to have gone in the other direction. By the looks of things, there was a dining room to the left of her, the thought of which was enough to make her stomach grumble. Straight in front was a corridor, with a long window at the end. For a moment, she stood there, trying to get her bearings, whilst thinking through the conversation she'd just had.

Was it strange that Giles had rung her, telling her to be nice? Probably not. Not if he guessed she would see the ring and start getting all judgy about it. But then, he had obviously changed it some time ago, and he could've easily spoken to her about it before now. Why wait until the minute she and Sienna were alone, or near enough? Was that odd? It felt odd.

With a deep breath in, she released a sound somewhere between a sigh and a groan. She had promised Giles, in the sweet shop, that their relationship wouldn't change now that he was engaged. That things would stay the same between them. But maybe Sienna was right. Maybe things couldn't stay the same. Maybe things had already changed. She'd certainly never doubted the truthfulness during her and Giles's conversations before.

Fingers crossed Faye had brought a couple more of those mini bottles of Prosecco with her. Although they'd probably have to ration them out. Even a small glass of bubbles on a stomach filled only with juice was a recipe for disaster.

Recalling what Sienna had said about wanting to have a dip in the pool before their dinner of mildly flavoured, probably green water, Holly turned around, ready to head back upstairs and get changed, when a series of squeals from outside caught her attention. Lots of squeals, followed by lots of laughter.

Intrigued as to what could cause such a reaction, Holly walked forward towards the window. With each step, the squealing got louder, although it was only when she was standing right there, by the pane of glass, that she saw exactly why the people were making so much noise. Her stomach sank.

'You have to be freaking joking,' she said.

34

Holly marched up the stairs, not once stopping her stride, even as she opened the door into her and Faye's room. She was so angry, she was trembling.

'Where have you been?' Faye said. 'You've been gone for ages.'

'I went to look around the resort.' Holly's voice hitched uncontrollably. 'I saw the spa.'

Faye grinned. 'Was it amazing? I was going to get my swimmers on, but this bed is so damn comfortable. I'll go down and check it out with you now.'

'I wouldn't get your hopes up if I were you,' Holly said. Her anger was turning into tears. She didn't know why it was making her so upset other than she'd given up a weekend with her daughter and friends and felt like she'd been tricked. Sienna had lied to her. This was as far away from a luxury spa weekend as she could ever imagine. 'It's a pond.'

'Sorry?' Faye frowned.

'The pool. It's not a pool at all. It's a pond.'

Faye's brow remained furrowed for a moment longer before her expression cleared. 'I don't think that's right.'

'It is. I saw it myself. It's labelled as a plunge pool. Only it's outside, surrounded by weeds, and there were ducks nesting at the edge of it. You know, this is a joke, right? This is all part of some weird game Sienna is playing.'

Faye stepped off the bed and walked towards Holly, who still hadn't moved from the doorway. She was too furious to move, her fists balled at her sides. Her jaw clicking as her teeth ground together.

'I'm sure it's just a misunderstanding?' Faye tried.

'What, like persuading Giles not to have children when we both know he desperately wants them? She's doing this deliberately. Making it seem like some great girly weekend where we can all relax and have a good time, when in actual fact, we're going to be half-starved and swimming in algae. Probably so we don't look too fat in her photographs. She is nuts. There is no way I'm going to be able to hold my tongue all weekend. She's a self-centred, narcissistic, manipulative bitch and I pray to God Giles sees the truth before it's too late.'

'Well, don't hold back, Holly,' a voice said behind her. 'Why don't you say how you really feel about me?'

35

Holly had never felt the blood drain from her body quicker. One moment, she had been filled with a red-hot anger, but then, upon hearing Sienna's voice, that all changed.

'Sienna...' Holly began, as she turned around to face her. Sienna was already shaking her head.

'No, no, I think you said everything you needed to say. What were the words you used? Manipulative, no, narcissistic. That was it, right? No, sorry, it was both, wasn't it?'

The warmth was returning to Holly's cheeks, but it wasn't anger. It was embarrassment. Then again, why was she feeling embarrassed? Hadn't Sienna brought them out here to this ridiculous place, knowing it would be like this? Before she could ask, Sienna carried on talking.

'You know what? I thought it would be a good chance for us to all refresh, to feel really good about our bodies and our minds. You know the waitlist for this place is over two years. *Two years*. They've turned away people like Willow and Sabrina because they didn't have space. And maybe I did think it would be good for you to get away from all that sugar you spend your day ingesting in the sweet shop. Was that so wrong of me? I thought you would enjoy it. I thought you would see that it was something special.'

Holly felt her jaw hanging open, but she was still struggling to find words. And unfortunately, Sienna had plenty.

'And as for the pond, you're right, there is a natural plunge pool, which has dozens of benefits, but I'm guessing you didn't go far enough to find the Olympic-length, heated swimming pool, three variations of sauna, and steam rooms?'

Her eyebrows were arched, and her cheeks sucked in so tightly, Holly could see her bone structure.

It was clear how she got so many rich people to part with their money. Holly would do anything to make that glare stop.

'Sienna—'

'No, no, I've had enough. Now, if you don't mind, I'm going down to the pool. The heated, indoor one. Faye—' Her gaze shifted from Holly for the first time since she had appeared. 'You're welcome to join me if you wish.' With a sniff, she looked back at Holly. 'I'm sure the concierge can arrange a taxi for you to go back to the station,' she said. 'Fingers crossed they have another train home tonight.'

36

Holly felt terrible. No, even terrible didn't come close to how she was feeling. It was horrific. The guilt in the pit of her stomach caused bile to sting the back of her throat while the rest of her body felt numb.

'Oh God,' she said. 'I was horrible, wasn't I? That was really, really bad, wasn't it?'

She looked at Faye, hoping that perhaps she would find some way to comfort her. Maybe say that it hadn't been as bad from the outside as it sounded to her. But all Faye could do was grimace. That said something, didn't it? When the most optimistic and nice-natured person she knew couldn't even muster a single lie for her?

'I just found the brochure with all the spa and sauna details,' she said. 'Probably a bit late for that now, isn't it?'

'Crap.'

Holly dragged herself inwards and dropped down onto the bed. 'Shit. Oh my God, Giles is going to kill me.'

Her guilt intensified with a memory of the phone call she'd had only moments before.

'Yeah, he's not gonna be too happy,' Faye said. 'But she might not tell him.'

Holly raised her eyebrows. Now she knew Faye was just trying to be comforting, even if she was massively lying. Sienna and Giles were engaged to be married, to spend the rest of their lives together. Of course, she was going to tell him. That was what a relationship like theirs meant.

'He told me I had to be nice,' she said. 'When he said it, I thought that was a ridiculous thing for him to say. Because I thought I was nice, but I'm not, am I? Oh my God. What do I do? What's best? I should go, shouldn't I? I should leave so that I don't ruin the rest of the weekend.'

She waited for Faye to respond, but when she did, it was with a withering look rather than words.

'What?' Holly said, trying to understand her expression. 'You don't think I should go?'

'Well,' Faith said, 'just answer this for me: would you be going because you don't want to ruin the rest of Sienna's weekend, or would you be going because it would be easier than having to apologise?'

'What?' Holly opened her mouth, ready to object to such a statement, only to realise it wasn't possible. As much as she didn't want to admit it to herself, Faye had hit the nail right on the head.

'So, what do I do? Just go down there and say I'm sorry? Say I didn't mean it?'

'Well, are you? Did you mean it or not?'

'Of course I'm sorry,' Holly said. 'It must have really hurt her to hear me say those things. I didn't want to do that.'

'Okay, but did you mean what you said? Because they're two different things.'

Holly grimaced. It was definitely frustrating having friends who were as logical-thinking as Faye, particularly when they were aiming that logic directly at her.

'I don't know. Truthfully... I don't know her. And the things she said about Giles and the kids, that was manipulative.'

'You're right, that was. But that's between them.'

'So you don't think he should know what she said? You don't think he has a right to know?'

'What I think is that right now, that isn't the issue. The issue you need to sort out first is you and Sienna. And yes, I do think that she can probably be a little manipulative, but not always in a bad way. She knows how to get what she wants. That's what she has to do in a job like hers, and for a very good cause. And maybe she should have told us about the juices, but my bet is that she didn't want us to be put off and she really wanted to spend some time with us. That's why she didn't say anything.'

Holly wouldn't have thought it was possible to feel any worse, and yet she did. Every word Faye had just spoke was true.

'You're right,' she said with a long sigh. 'I'll go find her now. Give me fifteen minutes before you come down to the pool. If I haven't come up by that time, I guess it means I'm not packing my stuff... but who knows?'

'Just be honest with her,' Faye said. 'I might not know her well, but most people value that.'

Holly nodded. 'Honesty, because that always works so well, doesn't it?'

37

Holly found Sienna by the pool. Just as she had said, it really was Olympic-sized, but it was no surprise Holly hadn't seen it before when she walked downstairs. It was on the other side of the building, with the saunas and steam rooms, the rest of the spa. Sienna had taken a lounger at the far end of the pool and was holding a book up to her face as if she was reading, though, in all the time it took Holly to walk across to her, not once did she seem to turn the page. She did, however, lift her hand to her eyes several times, as if she was wiping away tears. It was horrific; with every step closer Holly took, her guilt intensified. But there was nothing she could do about it.

It wasn't just guilt, though; it was nerves. Nerves about the impending apology she knew she had to make.

By the time she reached Sienna's sunlounger, her heart was hammering in its ribcage.

'Sienna. Can I have a word?'

Sienna sniffed before tilting her chin ever so slightly in Holly's direction. 'Have you come to tell me they've booked a taxi for you?'

'No,' Holly said. 'I haven't asked. I just... I was hoping we could have a conversation first.'

'Are you sure?' Sienna said. 'Why would you want to do that? I wouldn't want to have a conversation with anyone I thought was a narcissistic, manipulative bitch.'

Holly let out an internal groan. Sienna wasn't going to make this easy on her, but then what did she expect? She didn't deserve it to be made easy. Still, she wasn't going to give in. Giles would never forgive her. And so, steeling herself for the best result, she sat down on a sunlounger opposite Sienna.

'I am sorry,' she said. 'I really am.'

'Sorry because of what you said, or sorry because I heard you say it?' Sienna asked.

'Both,' Holly admitted. 'Look, the truth is, I don't know you. I don't. And it's all very well that you've gone to this extravagant effort for us, but I will admit, the idea of a juicing weekend for me is hell,' she continued. 'I'll be honest with you, I don't know anybody who would possibly think a weekend of juicing would be a fun holiday or bonding experience, but it's not just about that. Weekends are precious for me. I get to spend two a month with Hope. The other two, I'm normally working. Taking one entirely for myself is a rarity and so on the scarce occasion that I get a bit of time like this, I want to be spending it doing something I enjoy. Surely that makes sense to you?'

Sienna hummed. It wasn't much of a response, but it was something. Holly paused, took a breath in and carried on.

'But...' she said. 'That doesn't mean I was right in any way with what I said. I realise now that you like doing things like this, and that's why you thought we would enjoy it. I get that. But hopefully, you can see why I wasn't in the best possible mood when I saw the plunge pool?' Holly thought about the moments immediately preceding the plunge pool, where she spoke to

Giles. Faye may have said she needed to tell the truth, but telling Sienna about that didn't feel like the right thing to do.

While Holly waited for a reply, Sienna sniffed again.

'I asked Giles if he wanted to come with me, and he said no,' she said. 'And some other friends too. So maybe you're a bit right, and there's a bit of truth to what you say. Perhaps I did delay telling you what kind of spa it was, but that's only because I thought you'd come in with a negative attitude, and then when you got here, you'd absolutely love it. I'm sure you will. I mean, how can you not love it? Look at it.'

Holly looked around. 'You're right. It's lovely. At least for this part. But I'm using Uber Eats and getting a McDonald's at some point. I can tell you that now.'

Sienna let out a slight chuckle. 'Fair enough.'

For a second, Holly wondered if this was where she should end it. If this was the moment they should bring the conversation to a close, she would apologise, and they could carry on the weekend with some kind of unspoken, almost-resolution. But she couldn't. There was more she needed to say first.

'This has been harder for me than I expected it to be.'

Sienna laughed. 'You haven't even had your first juice yet; you might like it.'

Holly shook her head. 'I don't mean the juicing; I mean the engagement.'

'Oh, yes, I should probably have realised that.'

Holly sighed. 'I'll be honest. I didn't think Giles was ever going to be the settling-down type. I thought he would remain the eternal bachelor, and I would be the eternal widow, and that would work well in our little friendship group. But you changed that.'

'Giles will always be your very best friend. You're his best woman at the wedding, for crying out loud. I mean, who ever heard of such a ridiculous thing? Certainly not me. After all, it's going to make the photos look terrible. It'll completely ruin all the symmetry. Unless you wear a suit, I suppose.'

Holly wasn't sure whether or not that had been a genuine dig. There was no hint of a smile on Sienna's face, but even if she was serious, it was something they could deal with later. First, she needed to get all this out.

'The thing I'm finding hardest isn't about Giles and our friendship. I'm happy he's in love. Truly, but it scares me too. Because Giles marrying you means that life is moving on and there's absolutely nothing I can do to stop it. Either I move on too, or I spend the rest of my life trapped in the past, and I don't want to do that. I sure as hell don't want the others to do that either, but moving on... it's terrifying. But my fears are not something I should inflict on your life or your happiness. So I'm sorry. The way I acted, the things I said, they're not because of you, Sienna. They're really not. I would love it if we could use this weekend to get to know each other a little better.'

For the first time, Sienna finally lifted her sunglasses off her eyes and a small smile flickered on her face.

'I really think you will like the juices,' she said.

'I'm getting deliveries,' Holly replied with a laugh, and then, before she knew what was happening, Sienna had her arms wrapped tightly around her in a hug.

38

Holly managed to survive the entire first full day on juice alone. They were undeniably delicious and came with an apéritif of a Manuka honey and ginger shot, followed by a single spoonful of fresh raspberry sorbet for dessert.

Breakfast was a similar setup, although rather than a dessert, they also received three orange segments, two strawberries, two raspberries and four blueberries.

Insanely, Sienna wasn't a fan of strawberries and asked to swap.

'How could you not like strawberries?' Holly said on the Sunday morning. 'What about strawberry picking? That's literally the best thing in the world.'

'I've never been strawberry picking,' Sienna replied. 'You do it in fields, don't you?'

Holly's jaw dropped. 'What? That's ridiculous. You have to go. They should be opening them up in a couple of weeks again. You can come with Hope and me. We'll go plenty of times.'

'Really?' Sienna said, her eyes brightening. 'Will I get muddy?'

'We'll pick a nice day,' Holly said. 'Honestly, I am quite horrified.'

'I won't bring my two,' Faye said. 'We tried last year and Harry ate hundreds. Literally hundreds without me noticing. I only realised when we went to the counter to pay for what we had in our punnets and he threw up all over the grass. It was bright red. Obviously I lied and said he'd had a can of cherry aid before we came because I was terrified she was going to charge me double. I don't think I've ever been more mortified.'

'See, this is why I'm going to tell Giles we can't have children,' Sienna said. 'There is no way I could deal with that.'

Holly sucked back her response. She wasn't going to ruin the last day of the trip by saying something. Not now they were finally getting on well.

With all due credit to Sienna, the weekend had been a relaxation in a way Holly hadn't experienced for a long time. As well as spa treatments, the hotel also had a large range of board games, which the girls spent several hours playing together. Board games, Holly decided, were another great way to learn things about people. For example, she learned Faye was an absolutely terrible loser and would, if necessary, throw anybody under the bus to ensure she didn't come in last place. Sienna, on the other hand, liked to play dumb and pretend she didn't know what she was doing, even though she wiped the floor with them both several times.

But by the time Sunday morning came around, Holly was desperate for some proper food. Thankfully, so were Sienna and Faith.

'I think these are the best chips I've ever had in my life,' Faye said. They had been told surreptitiously by a member of staff that there was a local pub, a three-mile walk away. And it was a no-brainer for the lot of them.

'Maybe that's why these places are such hits,' Holly said as she dunked one of her salt-laden fries into a tub of homemade mayonnaise. 'Maybe they get you missing food so much that when you leave, everything in life feels better.'

Sienna raised her eyebrows. 'I don't know. I like the juices. Plus, those massages were amazing.'

Holly had to agree. 'They really were. Or at least I think mine was. I fell asleep in the first fifteen minutes. But I felt good when I woke up, so that's got to be something, hasn't it?'

The group chuckled.

'I'm not sure if I'm ready to go back to the real world tomorrow,' Faye said. 'It's been really nice, this switching off. Getting to know you guys.'

'It has,' Holly said, 'and I'm sorry again about the rocky start.'

Sienna waved a hand in the air nonchalantly. 'Honestly, all water under the bridge. But I am going to be roping you two in for a lot of wedding planning. I hope you know that.'

'I'm looking forward to it,' Holly said, in a way that sounded so convincing, she almost believed herself. She had got through a weekend with Sienna, and had got to know her so much better, just like she'd promised Jamie she would. But the more she had learned about Sienna, the more certain she was.

She and Giles were not right together, and somehow, he needed to see that.

39

Holly slept most of the journey back. It had been a long time since she had fallen asleep during a train journey, probably because she normally had Hope with her, but this time, she was out like a light. Her body was so relaxed, it was understandable she had difficulty staying awake, but there was another reason she closed her eyes in the first place. Sienna. The final few hours at the spa had been similar to the rest of the trip, with Sienna occasionally, and yet consistently, dropping in the odd lines here and there that made Holly see just how mismatched she and Giles were. Like when she said she'd probably give up work after they were married, even though she didn't want children, because Giles had more than enough money for both of them. Giles had one of the strongest work ethics Holly had seen. How did that match with Sienna's desire not to work at all? Still, she bit her tongue, only occasionally sharing a look with Faye, although she sometimes thought Giles's sister didn't hear half of the things Sienna said. She was too lost in her books, or swimming or occasionally worrying about home.

It would be up to Holly to raise the issues with Giles. She was sure of that. But she needed to tread carefully. Perhaps get Jamie's advice before she said anything.

As expected, Giles was there at the station to meet them.

As Holly stepped off the train, she picked up the pace to walk towards him, only to be overtaken by Sienna in a sprint. When she reached her fiancé, she jumped up into his arms and kissed him long and hard on the lips, while Holly stood awkwardly close behind.

'I can't believe how long the last couple of days have felt without you,' Sienna said.

'But I take it you had fun?' he asked.

'We had a wonderful time,' Sienna replied. 'Didn't we, girls?'

'We did,' they answered.

'It was a really special place,' Holly said, although Giles met her eyes for a split second longer than felt comfortable. She would need to tell him about the issue at the beginning of the weekend at some point, too, when Sienna had told her to leave, but that didn't feel like the moment to do it. It would be better to put it in context with other things Sienna had done, or rather said.

As soon as Holly got home, she texted Ben asking him to drop Hope off whenever worked. It didn't matter how many weekends she spent away from her daughter; there was always something special about coming home and seeing her.

So, when there was a knock on the door fifteen minutes later, she assumed it was the pair of them, but when she opened the door, Jamie was standing there with Rhubarb. The kitten had spent the weekend with Jamie's family and Holly was surprised to realise how much she had missed the small, furry addition to the family.

'Come here, you. Were you a good girl?' Holly said, as she took hold of her.

'Of course she was. Now, how did it go? I have to say, your text messages were amazing. Juicing. I mean, it would be funny for anyone, but with you and the sweet shop, it's absolutely hysterical.' Holly stood to the side, giving Jamie room to walk into the house. 'Let me guess, you had to sneak out and buy yourself a massive packet of custard creams to get you through.'

Holly chuckled. 'No custard creams, but we did go to the pub. We were very restrained, though – just a bowl of chips each. No burgers. No desserts.'

Jamie laughed. 'So, are you best buddies now?'

Holly offered her a look. 'No. Honestly, I don't know what I think of her. Except...'

'Except?'

Holly wanted to tell Jamie all the things Sienna had said over the weekend. All the ways she implied that money and a lavish lifestyle were her only requirements for a happy life, but she hesitated. Was Jamie just going to read into it? Assume Holly was saying this because of her latent feelings for Giles? Latent feelings that didn't exist. After all, Faye hadn't heard everything, and she was Giles's sister. She should have been studying and scrutinising Sienna even more than Holly. Besides, Hope was about to come home and she didn't want to get into a long discussion now.

'Nothing. She isn't entirely terrible,' she said eventually.

'Not entirely terrible, well that's better than it was,' Jamie said. 'I'm just gonna put on some food for the kids. Do you want me to put on Hope's too? Or are you having a night in, just the two of you?'

Holly breathed an internal sigh of relief that the conversation had moved so swiftly on from Sienna; she wasn't sure how long she would have managed to keep up the lying to Jamie.

'Dinner with you would be nice if that's okay,' Holly asked. 'I'm sure she's missed you guys as much as she's missed me.'

'Probably not. The kids and I went for a picnic with Georgia and the girls yesterday.'

Holly laughed. That was just the way their group was.

'Why don't I see what Hope wants to do, then? Is that okay?'

'Sure, just give me a message. I can always bung extra in the air-fryer if she wants to come over. Oh, and you know I'm going to need more actual details about the weekend, right?'

Holly rolled her eyes. 'Of course.'

Ten minutes later, Holly had all her washing in the machine when there was another knock on the door. This time, it was Hope.

'You don't mind if I— Do you?' Georgia said, still standing by the car. 'I've left Ben with the twins. It's been a pretty hectic weekend.'

'No, of course not. I'll see you soon,' Holly replied, but before she had even finished her sentence, Georgia was back in the car and reversing out of the driveway and Hope had her arms up, ready for a cuddle. There was no two ways about it. Hope gave the best cuddles in the world and even when Holly finally let her go, they continued to hold hands as they walked into the house.

'How was your weekend, sweetheart?' Holly asked.

'Good, better than Daddy's. Ivy was sick all over him.'

'Oh no, that doesn't sound good.'

'No, and it was just after Grace got chocolate all over the sofa too. That's why Georgia took us out to see Aunty Jamie.'

'Ahh, that makes sense. Now, Aunty Jamie said we could go round for dinner there if you want to,' she said. 'Or we can just stay in and watch a film together.'

'A film together sounds good,' Hope said and Holly felt a familiar warmth fill her heart. It was her strongest wish that Hope always loved spending time with her the way she did now. She wouldn't be able to bear it if they drifted apart as she grew up and would do whatever it took to stop that happening. 'Do I get to pick? Can we watch *Encanto* again? Actually, no. *Descendants Three*. No, *Descendants Four*. Can we watch all the *Descendants*?'

'Just go and find a film, all right?' Holly laughed. 'I'm going to make omelettes for dinner. Is that okay?'

Hope didn't reply. She had already disappeared into the living room, probably to put on the same film they had watched hundreds of times before. Holly was about to head into the kitchen when there was another knock at the door. She suspected that Jamie had seen Georgia drop off Hope and wanted to confirm the dinner plans, but when she opened the door, it wasn't Jamie there at all – it was Giles.

'Hey,' she said, 'is everything okay?'

'No,' he said, folding his arms across his chest. 'Everything is not okay. Not okay at all.'

Holly stepped back to look at Giles. It wasn't just that his arms were folded across his chest. His jaw was locked, his eyes were blazing and there was even a little vein pulsing on his forehead; he was absolutely fuming.

'Giles—'

'Uncle Giles!' Before Holly could get a word out, Hope was out of the living room, her arms tight around Giles's waist. For a split second, he allowed his anger to drop as he looked down at her.

'Hopey bear, could you do me a massive favour and go into Aunty Jamie's? I just need to have a word with your mum.'

'I'm watching _Descendants_. I think we're going to watch _Descendants Three_. You can watch with Mum and me if you want. Mum really likes it, don't you?'

Giles smiled at her, but Holly could see the way his lips were twitching, the tightness trembling in the expression.

'That sounds good. Maybe another night, but right now, your mum and I need to have some grown-up talk. And it really would be a massive favour to me if you could just pop next door. I know that Jamie was saying she wanted your help too.'

Hope shifted her gaze between Giles and Holly several times, but she didn't move.

'How much do you want me to go next door?' she asked. 'Enough to pay me?'

'Hope!' Holly said in shock. 'Your Uncle Giles just said he needed you to go next door, so do it, please. Or there'll be no film.'

'Fine,' Hope said. A moment later, she was out the front door, knocking on Jamie's. It wasn't until Holly heard her disappear inside that she looked back at Giles.

'I'm guessing Sienna said something about the slight misunderstanding we had at the beginning of the weekend,' she said. There was no point denying it; after all, she'd been planning on telling him, anyway. 'I was going to tell you when we got a chance to speak alone,' she added, stepping into the house. 'Actually, there are a few things I wanted to talk to you about. A few things to do with Sienna.'

Nerves churned within her. This wasn't the way Holly had planned on having this conversation. She had wanted time to work out how to word things. Not to mention make a comprehensive list of all Sienna's snide comments, so she didn't forget anything, but she was just going to have to wing it.

'Do you want a cup of tea? Or something stronger?' she asked.

Giles didn't speak; he hadn't said a single word since he'd sent Hope out of the house, and the silence was even more unnerving than yelling.

'I asked you…' he said finally. 'I asked you to be nice. To get to know her. She arranged this for you—'

'I know, Giles, but—'

'And if half of what she's told me is true, then—'

'Half? What do you mean? I said one wrong thing at the start of the trip and apologised.'

'Really? What about demanding everyone went to the pub because you refused to eat another juice?'

'What?' Holly's jaw dropped. 'That's not what happened at all. And I'm not sure you can eat juice but—'

'And what about calling her, what was it, a narcissistic bitch?'

That one Holly couldn't deny, but he still hadn't got it right.

'It was actually a manipulative, narcissist—' Holly began, before clamping her mouth shut.

'You are a piece of work,' Giles said, his voice rising.

'Me? You don't know the half of it. She's not right for you, Giles. You don't understand—'

'What I don't understand is why I actually thought you might be happy for me. That you might see that this is what you want.'

Though she wouldn't have thought it previously possible, Giles was even more angry than he had been when he arrived.

She stepped forward and, despite the rage that filled her, softened her voice as much as she could.

'I get that you want to settle down, Giles. I know you want to find someone to spend the rest of your life with. But not her. If you'd just let me tell you—'

'Stop it, Holly. Please, haven't you already caused enough hurt? Sienna was in floods of tears. You know that? She was devastated.'

'No, she wasn't,' Holly said. It was obvious Sienna had portrayed her as this massive villain, and she wasn't having it. Not when she had actually spent the weekend making an effort. 'She was hurt, yes. But only immediately after the incident. Afterwards, I went straight down to the pool. You can ask Faye. She was the one who told me I should go and speak to her. Apologise.'

'My sister had to tell you to apologise for calling my fiancée a bitch? Great going there, Holly. Brilliant.'

'Will you just listen to me!' The calm Holly had tried to portray was gone. 'I apologised to her. I told her how difficult this is for me. How difficult you moving on, and everyone moving on with their lives, is for me. We got past it, okay? And everyone wanted to go to the pub. We'd had nothing but juice for over a day! Ask Faye. You know me, Giles. You know I wouldn't be like that. That I would never deliberately hurt anyone.'

'I don't know what to believe right now, but the fact you would say anything that horrible to her makes me think I don't know you, Holly. Not like I thought I did.'

The words felt like a knife in her chest. Never for one second had Holly believed Giles would take Sienna's word over hers.

Tears filled her eyes. 'Don't say that. It's not true.'

'People change, Holly.'

'But you said we wouldn't. You said nothing would change between us.'

No one was shouting now. Instead, it was a painful silence that gripped the room.

'Maybe I was wrong.' His throat rose and fell visibly as he swallowed. 'I have to choose Sienna. She has to come first from now on.'

'Please, Giles...' Holly couldn't tell him what kind of person Sienna really was. He wouldn't believe her. Not now. She could feel it. And so, rather than speaking, she stepped forward and placed a hand on his chest. She had made the motion hundreds of times in their friendship, just like she'd held his hand hundreds of times or rested her head on his shoulder. But something about it felt different.

'I don't know what I'd do without you.'

'What do you want me to say, Holly?'

She didn't know. There wasn't an answer she could give. They were incredibly close now, only inches apart, and her eyes tried to lock on his. But for some reason, they kept flickering down towards his lips. Why couldn't she stop looking at his lips?

'We'll get through this,' he said finally. 'It'll just take some time. I promise.'

'I don't think you can promise that,' she whispered. 'I think things have already changed. For both of us.'

There was a strange buzzing on the surface of her skin. A static-type feeling. Was Giles sensing it, too? By the way his pupils filled his irises as he looked at her, she had to believe he did.

'Life has to move on at some point, Holly,' he whispered.

'I know. I know it does.'

She was moving onto her tiptoes, although she wasn't exactly sure why.

'I don't know how I'd manage without you in my life, Holly.' His voice was a breath so warm against her skin, she wanted to breathe it all in. She needed to.

'You won't ever have to find out. Like you said, we'll get through this.'

'We will?'

'We will.'

Then, in a heartbeat, before Holly could work out what was happening, the space between them had closed entirely, and for the first time in a decade, Holly Berry and Giles Caverty were kissing.

41

Holly couldn't remember moving. She couldn't remember putting her lips against his, but nor could she remember Giles putting his lips against hers. It was as if they had been drawn together and now that they were, it felt like the most natural thing in the world. Like this was how they were meant to be. She felt the hitch in her heart and the quickening of her breath as her hand reached up around the back of his neck. At the same time, he slid his hand around her waist, pulling her in closer. Every inch of her body was on fire. The static buzz now full-on sparks on her skin. How was this so easy? How did it feel so right? It made little sense, but at the same time, it did. She was kissing Giles. She was kissing her best friend Giles. Her best friend Giles, who was engaged to the horrific Sienna.

'Stop!' She jumped back away from him, her hands outstretched in front of her. 'Sienna—'

'Oh my God,' he said. 'Why did you do that?'

'What?'

Holly had meant to tell him about all the things Sienna had said. That was what she suddenly remembered. That, and the fact that he was an engaged man and there was no reason in the world that she should be kissing him regardless of how vile his fiancée was. He needed to know the truth, yet Giles's hand was covering his mouth like he had just done the most hideous thing ever. And he had blamed her for it.

'What the hell was that?' Giles said.

'That was... I think it was both of us,' Holly said. 'I think that we... I think that we...'

'No.' Giles was shaking his head as he paced back and forth across the room. 'No. We can't have done that. You shouldn't have done that. We can't. I love her. I love her, and I know I'm going to marry her. I know that. It was just... it was just some weird moment. You were angry, and I was angry, and—'

'You're right, it was just an angry kiss,' Holly said quickly.

'Yes, yes, exactly,' Giles agreed, striking the air with his hand. 'It was just an angry kiss. Those happen, right? You were just angry and upset, and I was there. That's all it was. I was just there.' He brushed himself down, at the same time as trying to wipe his mouth, like he was attempting to erase any hint of a kiss from his lips. 'I need to go. Yes, I should go. I need to go back to my fiancée.'

'Giles, we...' She paused. She wouldn't be able to get through to him like this. She could tell.

'Can we talk later?' she asked, but there was no point. He had already turned around and was marching away from her.

A second later, the front door slammed shut.

42

Holly wasn't sure how long she'd been sitting there. She was determined not to move until she knew what she was going to do next, and how on earth could she know what she was going to do next when it still didn't make sense to her what she'd already done? She had kissed Giles. That was what he'd said anyway, but she didn't believe that. She had been there. She had seen the way his body moved towards her. Felt the way he pulled her closer into him. She had been the one to break away. That she was certain of. And that had to count for something, right?

As she buried her head in her hands, all she could see was Giles's face after the moment. The way he had looked so appalled. Disgusted even. Because they had kissed. It was such an absolute mess.

With a sudden burst of focus, she picked up her phone. She needed to ring him. She needed to put things straight. That was what she needed to do. Yet how could she ring him when Sienna was probably there? It didn't matter how much she disliked the woman; it didn't change what Holly had done, and that wasn't the type of conversation Giles would be able to have with her in the room, was it?

As a new surge of panic kept her pulse unhealthily fast, Rhubarb appeared at her ankles, meowing softly.

'I think Mummy might have messed this up. Badly,' she said to the cat. 'What do you think I should do? I have to do something, right?'

Rhubarb meowed again. It wasn't the most conclusive answer, but it was as close as she was going to get to one.

So, what about a text? She switched from phone calls to open up a message but struggled to know what to write.

Sorry we kissed? No, she definitely couldn't put something like that in a text. What if Sienna saw it appear on his phone? No, that wasn't a great idea. So, if she couldn't ring or message, what could she do? She didn't know, but she was still staring at her phone when it started buzzing in her hand.

'Oh God!' she said, as she jumped so high, she accidentally threw it up into the air. Had Giles beaten her to it? Was he ringing her? If so, he was going to expect her to say something when she didn't know what the hell she could say. The phone landed face down on the sofa beside her, still buzzing. Did it normally sound this angry when it buzzed? She didn't think so. Regardless, it was showing no signs of stopping. She had no choice but to answer it.

With her throat so dry she could barely swallow, Holly inched towards the phone, then flicked it over with one finger, like it was some dead thing she didn't want to touch. When she saw Jamie's name flashing on the screen, her whole body groaned with relief.

'Hey,' she said, still waiting for her pulse to lower as she answered the call.

'Hey, what's going on?'

And just like that, it was rising again.

'What do you mean, what's going on?' she said. 'Nothing is going on. Why do you think something is going on? I'm fine. Nothing is going on here at all. Why do you sound as if you think something was going on?'

Holly clamped her mouth shut.

'Okay, that was very, very weird,' Jamie said. 'I'm here with Hope. She said Giles came over, and we assumed you were going to come back and get her, but that was over half an hour ago. Is everything all right? Did something happen between you and Giles?'

'What do you mean?'

'I don't know. You're just behaving strangely.'

Holly let out a deep sigh. Should she tell Jamie? She floated the idea, only momentarily, before she pushed it away again. Jamie was close to Giles now, just as she was to Ben and every other member of the group. It didn't make sense to bring anybody else into the situation. Not when it meant she would have to lie or hide things from them.

Besides, there was something else Holly could say. A half-truth.

'Sienna and I had a bit of an argument. A bust-up on the first day there.'

'What? Why didn't you say anything? What did you do?'

'It wasn't that big a deal. Or at least, I didn't think it was. But then Sienna went home to Giles crying about it. Obviously, he wasn't happy, so he wanted to check that stuff was okay, to clear the air and things.'

'And did you do that? Did you manage to clear the air?'

Holly closed her eyes, only for an image of Giles's lips pressed against hers to fill her mind. She could still feel the way his hand had slipped around her waist and how her fingers had toyed with the hair at the nape of his neck. She could almost feel the rhythm of his pulse too, they had been that close.

With a sharp breath in, Holly snapped her eyes back open again.

'Yes, sort of... yes, yes. Everything is fine. Completely fine.'

'Okay then, so do you want me to give Hope dinner here or send her back around to you?'

Holly thought about the question for a second longer.

'I've just got a couple of errands to run. I'll come around to you in fifteen minutes. Is that okay?'

'Yeah, sure. Are you sure you're all right? You sound strange.'

'That's what a juicing weekend will do to you,' Holly said. 'Honestly, I think I probably just need some sugar. I'll be over in a minute.'

'Sure thing. I'll get the wine ready.'

As Holly hung up the phone, a sharp tug of guilt yanked at her chest. That was probably the most she'd lied to any of her friends in a very, very, very long time.

Almost nothing she'd said had been true, apart from the bust-up with Sienna and it being her fault. She and Giles had definitely not cleared the air. In fact, they'd never had more things they needed to discuss, but she couldn't send a text, and she couldn't phone him either, so what choices did that leave? A letter didn't feel right either. A letter would require delivering and would be a tangible piece of evidence of everything that had gone on. But then, maybe there was another way after all. Another way she could get down everything she needed to say.

'I guess I'm sending an email,' she said to Rhubarb, who had begun pouncing on a stray hair tie Hope had left lying about.

Moving over to the desk, she opened up her laptop and began to write. It wasn't as easy as she had hoped. A myriad of thoughts flowed through her mind, but she didn't know where to start. If she started with what a bitch Sienna was, Giles might think she was diverting the attention away from herself, like she wasn't to blame and she didn't feel responsible for what had happened. Then again, she was happy to take half the blame, but not all of it. There was no way she would take all the blame. After all, there were two people involved in that kiss and as far as she was concerned, Giles had initiated it just as much as she had. But how did she say that without implying he was a terrible person who cheated on his fiancée, unless she mentioned how horrible Sienna was? It was a catch-22.

'Why is this so hard?' she said, dropping her head into her hands. She and Giles talked about everything. He was her go-to person. Why was it so difficult to tell him the truth in this situation? A deep throbbing began behind her ribs. Perhaps, she thought, it was because she didn't want to admit the truth to herself. She couldn't admit the truth, could she?

It was then that her fingers started writing. Not much. Barely even a sentence. Just seven short words. Seven short words that felt like freedom. That felt like releasing a rope that had bound her in place for longer than she'd even realised. Seven short words that would upset everything.

'Who'm I kidding?' she said as Rhubarb jumped onto her lap. 'There's no way I can send that. That would just make things more complicated. A lot more complicated.'

With a heavy sigh, she read through the sentence once more before shaking her head and lifting her arm. She hadn't realised until that moment that Rhubarb had her back legs balanced on her, and that by shifting her position even slightly, Holly left the kitten with no choice but to move. In the split second, as she went to press the delete button, Rhubarb jumped onto her keyboard and her small paw hit the mouse. At any other time, that might not have been an issue. Only the cursor was hovering directly over the send button, and the minute the mouse was pushed, it clicked.

'No!' Holly squealed as she saw the moment unfolding, but it was too late. The email had gone. Giles knew exactly how she felt.

43

Holly couldn't fall asleep.

She tried, but every two minutes, she was struck with the urge to check her phone and see if Giles had messaged her – a text, an email, a missed call, anything at all. But there was nothing. Maybe it was because he knew, like she did, that it couldn't possibly be true, could it? She didn't *actually* love him, did she? She had just written the words down, that was all. She hadn't had any intention of him seeing them.

With a loud groan, Holly covered her face with her hands. Why had she even written it in an email? That had to be the worst option of all; there was no way of telling whether he'd read it. Maybe she should ring him now. Would it be that unusual? She'd rung him late at night before. Sometimes for specific reasons, like when a thought had struck, and she didn't want to forget it, or she wanted to ask him a question, but other times, she just wanted to talk, and he was the one person she knew wouldn't mind being woken up in the middle of the night just to listen to her.

But that was different. He wasn't engaged then. Sienna would be there if she rang him now. Sienna, who lied. Sienna, who was, just as Holly had said, a manipulative narcissist, and Holly didn't want her anywhere within earshot when she spoke to Giles and told her exactly what type of woman he was planning on marrying. Then again, what type of woman was *she*? Holly's anger turned inwards. It was all very well pointing out Sienna's faults, but it didn't change that she was the type of person who kissed another woman's fiancé; that was who.

She sat bolt upright in bed, as another thought struck. What if he'd already told Sienna? It wasn't beyond the realms of possibility. After all, Sienna had told him about the argument – or at least her version of it. Who was to say Giles wouldn't be bound by loyalty and need to get it off his chest the second he saw her? Oh God. Holly could feel the panic starting again. What was she going to say to Sienna if she did turn up? She couldn't deny it, obviously. That would make her look crazy. But if she started a tit for tat with all the things Sienna had done, had said, then she'd just look bitter and jealous.

Besides, she refused to take all the blame. She was the one who had broken away. How long would they have gone on kissing for if she hadn't stopped? And who was to say kissing was all they would have done? The thought made her feel simultaneously dizzy and nauseous. She could not think about doing those things with Giles Caverty. It was a one-off, an accident, and it would never happen again. She was positive. It was just like she'd said to Sienna: all this crazy change was doing something strange to her. That was why it had happened. So what about the words she wrote in the email? The email she hadn't planned on sending. Yes, that was just another moment of unbalanced thinking. She would go to sleep, wake up in the morning and feel absolutely back to normal. That was the plan, at least.

* * *

'You're coming over to Ben and Georgia's today, aren't you?' Jamie said when she popped into the sweet shop around midday.

'Ben and Georgia's? Why are we going there? It's a Monday.'

'They sent a message saying they wanted to have a barbecue, you know. First barbecue of the year and everything. Everybody's going.'

'Everybody?'

'Well, you know… Caroline and Ian, Sienna and Giles—'

'I've got loads of tax work stuff to do,' Holly said.

'Taxes?' Jamie replied. 'You did your taxes last month. UK taxes are due in April, remember?'

'Yes, yes, absolutely.' Holly could feel the heat rising up through her neck. 'It's just… obviously, April, June… I need to make sure I don't make the same mistakes I did last year. I promised the accountant. I had a load of things muddled. Really boring… just dates and numbers. Lots and lots of numbers.'

'Numbers, for an accountant? That's unusual,' Jamie said. Her eyes narrowed. 'There's something going on.'

'No, no, not at all. It's just… you know how tax is. I don't suppose you'll be able to drive Hope across with you? Or I can drop her off and pick her up again. Or Ben can. She might want to stay with Ben. I'll check with Ben. That's the best thing to do.'

'You're babbling,' Jamie said as a large crease formed between her eyebrows. 'Something going on.'

'No, nothing is going on at all. I just said that I've got the tax stuff to do.'

Holly simultaneously shuffled and shook her head, resulting in an action that looked like a jellyfish trying to shimmy.

For a second longer, Jamie stayed exactly where she was, before a wide grin broke on her face.

'Oh my God,' she said. 'I know what it is.'

Holly's muscles tightened. 'No, you don't. There's nothing to know. What do you think you know?'

'You've had enough of Sienna?' she said. 'You're pretending that everything was great, but one whole weekend and you're needing some respite from her. You're worried she's going to go all "best buddies" on you.'

Holly let out a nervous chuckle that was tight and high-pitched and strained in her throat.

'Yes, yes, that's exactly what it is. I just… I need a little bit of a break – you understand, don't you? It was quite a full-on weekend.' It wasn't a lie. Not exactly. She had no desire to see Sienna again, but definitely not with Giles at her side.

'Sure, no worries. We'll probably take both cars anyway, as Fin's going to come out later, so he can drive Hope back. If you're all right with that?'

'Thank you,' Holly said, letting out a sigh of relief.

But Jamie continued to stare at her.

'You know you're not going to be able to avoid Sienna forever, don't you?' she said.

Holly's smile tightened. 'Of course, of course,' she said. 'Honestly, everything'll be fine. Completely fine.'

And yet, even as she spoke, she had no idea how that could possibly be true.

44

Holly was aware that not everybody saw their friends as much as she did. After all, she worked with Caroline, lived next door to Jamie, and shared a daughter with Ben. It was understandable that they would spend a fair amount of time together, but for the next two weeks, she did everything within her power to avoid seeing them. As well as missing Ben's first barbecue of the year, she also skipped out on the picnic Caroline arranged at the Slaughters, the group family cycle ride Michael was in charge of, which ended with them all going to a pub and having a very wobbly ride home, and a foraging trip arranged by Fin. Her excuses were getting weaker and weaker; she knew that. And more than once, Jamie had tried to question her.

'Something obviously happened with Sienna,' Jamie pressed. 'I don't know why you won't tell me what it is. You know I'd take your side on it. That's what best friends do.'

'I've just got a lot going on. It's nothing,' Holly lied. She didn't even want to tell Jamie the truth about how Sienna had commented about not actually wanting children, or lying to Giles about Holly forcing them all to the pub. If she did that, she would find herself in an even deeper conversation, and then the truth of what happened between her and Giles might come out and she couldn't let that happen.

But despite what Jamie said, she knew there was no way she could take Holly's side when it came to the kiss. Holly was very, very definitely in the wrong there.

'Okay, you're still doing the baking for Sunday, aren't you?' Jamie said as she came round and sat in Holly's kitchen two weeks after the event.

'Baking for Sunday?' Holly asked.

'It's the twins' naming day, remember? Honestly, where have you been the last couple of weeks? You know all this. That's why Fin's picking up his mum from the airport tomorrow.'

'Oh God, yes, of course. The twins' naming day. Right. You wanted cakes, right? Cupcakes?'

'Yes, but you were going to do biscuits and things too. I thought you were going to do as much as you can – at least, that's what you did for Randall's, right?'

'Yes, of course I did. Of course, I'll do the same, yes, absolutely. No problem at all.'

Holly wrote a large note, which she stuck on the fridge. It wasn't like her to need reminders for things as big and important as Jamie's children's naming days, but currently, her mind was stuck and was only able to focus on one specific incident. An incident that had happened in this very kitchen.

'It's a man, isn't it?' Jamie suddenly burst out with.

Holly spun around. 'What? What do you mean?'

'That's the reason you're so distracted. Of course it is! I don't know why I didn't see it before. You're away with the fairies the entire time and you're never free to meet up with everyone. It's so you can sneak off and have a bit of time with whoever this person is, isn't it? Oh my God, I need to know everything. Tell me now, tell me who it is!'

Holly could feel her cheeks colouring, a heat flooding through the whole of her body.

'It's not... it's not what you think,' she said. 'I'm not seeing anyone.'

Jamie raised an eyebrow. 'You're not gonna get away with that with me. I know you.'

She was right: Holly knew that. Once Jamie had an idea in her head, there was no way she'd let it go. So what choice did that leave Holly with? Tell the truth? No, there was no way she could do that.

'It's nothing really, just a couple of dates,' she said.

'Oh my God!' Jamie's face split into a smile so broad, it caused a crack to break in Holly's heart. 'I need to know everything! Now. Right now.'

'There's really nothing to know,' Holly said. 'It's just a guy who came into the sweet shop a couple of times and asked if I fancied a drink.'

'A sweet-shop customer? Does that mean Caroline knows him too? Oh my God, I have to hear everything. Does she know?'

'No, no, please. This is all very new, and it's nothing. It's really nothing. I don't like the guy even. I know I don't. It's just... you guys were pestering me so much about dating that I thought I'd give it a go. But it was a stupid idea, and he's arrogant and stubborn and definitely not the right type of person for me to be with.'

'Wow, you really have formed a strong opinion of this guy after a couple of dates.'

Holly felt the red deepen. 'Well, I just thought I needed to give it a fair chance. But there's no point; there's really not. It won't go anywhere at all.'

For a moment, Jamie looked at her, and Holly wondered what she was going to say. She prayed to God she wouldn't ask for more, as she had no idea how to get herself out of that problem. Instead, Jamie stepped forward and took Holly by the hands.

'I'm proud of you,' she said. 'I know that couldn't have been easy. And if you don't like this guy, then move on. You know better than any of us that life is too short to spend with someone who doesn't have your whole heart. But I'm really proud of you.'

The guilt was so intense, Holly didn't know how she wasn't consumed by it entirely. She felt guilty for lying to Jamie, guilty for having been a terrible friend and avoiding everybody, but most of all, guilt because of Giles. Guilt because of that email she had sent. Those words she had written down. Words she was struggling to deny even more than ever.

Her throat thickened with tears, but she blinked them away.

'I should head back,' Jamie said. 'Fin was painting skateboards with the boys, so I should really check how much of a state the house is in now.'

'No worries,' Holly said. 'I'll make a list of things for the naming day.'

'Fantastic. Thank you. See you later.'

It was only as Jamie stepped outside onto the patio that another thought struck Holly.

'Jamie,' she said. 'Who are the twins' guide-parents? It would be nice to know, just to make some personalised biscuits for them.'

'Oh, did I not tell you?' she said. 'Caroline and Michael, Fin's cousin Laura and Giles.'

'So Giles is going to be there on Sunday?' Holly said, a familiar heat filling her face.

Jamie let out a laugh as she waved her hand and walked away. 'Dating puts you in the strangest mood,' she said.

45

Holly kept her mind on her baked goods. It was a fabulous distraction. That and ensuring she was as indispensable and helpful as possible throughout every moment of the naming-day ceremony. By busying herself in that way, she didn't have time to speak to anybody. Let alone think about the damn kiss that continued to plague her every waking moment. That was the plan, at least. But the later in the day it got, the harder it was to keep herself separate from everybody. And by everybody, she meant Giles and Sienna.

'Holly, come on, we need some photos,' Jamie said.

'I'll be there in a second,' Holly said.

'No. Come now. This second. You already missed the first round.'

They had chosen a beautiful riverside area off the beaten track for the ceremony. It was a hippyish affair – at least, that was how Holly's mother had referred to it. But Holly loved the informality of the day, the fun, the children playing, running wild. The photos she had from Randall's naming day were some of her favourites, and they were filled with the best memories – memories that were a lot harder to create today, given how tense she was.

'I just want to make sure the wasps and ants don't get to the food,' Holly said. 'I'll stay over here.'

'You are being ridiculous,' Jamie said. 'We can't have a photo without you in it. They'll be fine for five minutes.'

Grumbling, Holly found a couple of serviettes, which she draped over the food before traipsing over to join the others.

'About time,' Jamie said. 'Now come on. Squeeze in next to Giles.'

'I'll come and stand next to Hope,' Holly said.

'No, I've got a height thing going on. Come on, just squeeze in there. It'll work much better.'

'Sorry,' Holly muttered as she squeezed herself in between Sienna and Giles.

She could feel her face glowing with embarrassment. 'Do you really want me to go in between Sienna and Giles? Surely couples should be together.'

'Not for this they don't have to be. It works. Trust me.'

Holly was fully aware of the glares she was receiving from both sides as she wriggled into the gap, but while she couldn't give a monkey's how Sienna was looking at her, Giles's glower caused a deep throbbing behind her sternum.

'Sorry, I just—'

'It's fine,' he snapped.

It's fine. Those were the first two words Giles had spoken to her in two weeks. What was he referring to? The fact that she had to press up close to him to get in the photo, or the email she'd sent, or the kiss? Was that what was fine? Or maybe it had nothing to do with that – maybe it was just because she'd had to jostle them out of the way a bit so that she could fit in the photo.

'Okay, everybody get ready to say *naming day*!' Jamie called out as she set the phone on a timer. 'Here we go: three, two, one, naming day!'

Several of the children pulled funny faces at the exact moment the camera went off, but Holly wouldn't have expected anything else.

'Okay, a couple more with the guide-parents, then we'll get to the food.'

Holly let out a sigh of relief – at least she didn't have to be involved in that. That had to be the most difficult bit done, right? Now she could just avoid people she didn't want to speak to and try to leave early. Maybe she could say she needed to see her parents. Yes, that would be the perfect excuse. After all, her mum had been struggling more and more recently.

She was just checking the time and wondering how long she would have to wait before making her excuses when a voice spoke to her.

'Holly?'

She turned around; her stomach somersaulted. Sienna was there, looking straight at her.

'Sienna?' Holly knew her voice sounded strained.

'It's been so long. It feels like it's been so long,' Sienna said, reaching her arms around Holly and squeezing her tightly. 'You know, the spa feels like weeks ago, doesn't it?'

'Well, it was two weeks ago.'

'I know, but I mean weeks and weeks ago. And I need to apologise. I really hadn't planned on telling Giles about our little tiff. We just share everything. You know what that's like? You've been in relationships.'

'I have,' Holly replied, feeling a familiar twitch along her jaw. 'The type where you actually tell the truth to one another. I was

surprised to hear that *I* demanded to go to the pub. I hadn't
realised.'

Sienna didn't so much as bat an eyelid.

'You can't say you gave us much choice, can you really? Come
on, your entire apology finished with saying you were going to
get McDonald's delivered.'

'It was a joke. As you know.'

'Hmm, and did anyone find it funny?'

Holly wasn't going to put up with it any longer. Sienna was
nothing more than a schoolyard bully, only they weren't in
school any more. She was a grown-up and if she thought she was
going to push Holly out of her friendship groups, not to mention
out of Giles's life, she was very much mistaken.

'I know you think you know what you're doing, but you're not
going to come out on top of this.' Holly's voice trembled.

'I don't know, I was on top last night, and the night before. Or
is that not what you mean?' Sienna smirked. 'You really are
an im—'

'Oh my God, I love these days. It makes me want to have
another baby.'

Holly turned around to see Caroline standing there, with one
of Holly's naming-day biscuits in her hand.

Holly turned back to look at Sienna. Her blood was boiling.
Had Sienna really just made that comment? And again, with no
one there to hear. And now Holly couldn't even respond. Not
with Caroline there. Sienna would just return to being as nice as
pie and Holly would look crazy if she said or did anything.

'So, what are you talking about?' Caroline said. 'Wedding
stuff? It must be so exciting. It feels like decades since ours. Actually, it was decades.'

Sienna offered a trite little titter that anybody in their right
mind could tell was fake, but Caroline smiled.

'So, how's it all going? There must be loads to sort out.'

'You have no idea.' Sienna rolled her eyes. 'I know it's just one day, and it's not what matters, is it? Even if everything goes wrong, it'll still be a perfect day because I'm marrying the perfect man.'

'Oh my God, you are so sweet,' Caroline cooed. 'Aren't they so sweet, Holly?'

'Sickeningly so,' Holly replied.

Sienna shot her a glower before she continued. 'There's just so much to sort out. I'm trying to get the same photographer that Meghan and Harry had. I absolutely adored the photographs. And then there's the flowers. I think a wedding can be ruined by bad flowers, don't you? They're basically the cornerstone of all the photos. It's not just the professional photos you have to think of, after all. It's all the guests who post them online. Good flowers can make such a difference to how the images look.'

'What happened to "everything is perfect as long as you're marrying the perfect man"?' Holly muttered under her breath, yet once again, Sienna ignored her comment.

'There's a florist I follow online,' she said. 'Everything he does is phenomenal. It would be my absolute dream to have him do the wedding. He's got an exhibition in Anglesey, just for two days starting tomorrow and I'm desperate to go, but I've got an event at work I just can't get out of. It's such a shame. I'm heartbroken, if I'm honest. I mean, I adore the photos he posts, but you never know how edited they are, do you? I really need to see what they're like in real life. But Anglesey? It's a four-hour drive. It would take a whole day just to go there and back.'

'And you can't get someone to cover for you?' Caroline asked.

'Mine isn't the type of job where you can just get someone to cover you,' Sienna said. Everything about her was so damn patronising, Holly wanted to hit her. She didn't know how she was managing not to.

'That's such a shame,' Caroline said, seemingly oblivious to the complete condescending manner in which she'd been spoken to. 'Why don't you see if there's someone who can go up for you? Take photos? That way, you'd know if they were edited or not.'

'It's a great idea, but I'd have to find someone I could really trust.'

'Well, I'm working at the sweet shop, but Holly is off. And I'm sure Giles is free. The pair of them could go up together, couldn't they? There couldn't be two people you trust more to take some photos, could there?'

Holly watched as a smile tightened on Sienna's lips.

'Well, I'm not sure it will be that simple. Photos are tricky to get right. The light and composition...'

'But if you really want to know what they would look like unedited, like the guests would take at the wedding, then it would be better to have normal people go, wouldn't it? Isn't that what you just said?'

'I understand what you're saying, only... only—'

Sienna was clearly trying to figure out a way out of the situation, and Holly desperately wanted to see what excuse she came up with, but Caroline was already waving her hand.

'Giles! Giles, you haven't got anything sorted for tomorrow, have you?'

Slowly he ambled over towards them.

'Is everything okay?' Giles asked. Holly wished her stomach would stop the strange fluttering churning it had begun, but she also wished Giles would at least look in her direction and stop pretending she didn't exist. Although that was what she had been trying to do all day too.

'Sienna wants someone to go and take some photos of these flowers she likes tomorrow,' Caroline said. 'Are you free?'

'I can be.'

Sienna shifted a little. 'It's really not that important.'

'A minute ago, you said that they were the most perfect flowers possible, and you were heartbroken you couldn't go,' Caroline said.

'I'm not sure I worded it like that.'

'Those were exactly your words.'

Holly wanted to hug Caroline. At least someone else was seeing a tiny snippet of Sienna's fakeness. Caroline would be the person Holly finally told about the things Sienna had said at the spa and after this, she would believe her. She knew it. Feeling a sense of elation, Holly opened her mouth, ready to back Caroline up and say that those were, indeed, the words Sienna used, but before she could, Giles was speaking.

'Is that right?' he said. 'You want to see this florist?'

'I am a big fan of his work,' Sienna replied eventually. 'But there'll be others, I'm sure.'

'She can't go and get photos. She wants some unedited ones, so I suggested you and Holly go and take some. Sounds like a perfect idea, don't you think?'

Holly knew what Giles was going to say. Of course she did. There was no way he would agree to something as ridiculous as an eight-hour round trip alone with Holly when the last time they had been together, they had ended up kissing. He was going to say no and that was what she wanted him to say, wasn't it? It was the right thing to say.

She looked at him, and for the first time all day, he finally met her gaze. Without warning, her chest began to flutter in a manner she had not believed was possible any more. Could he feel it too? He could. Somehow, she knew this wasn't in her head. It wasn't all on her. He could feel it too.

All of a sudden, the answer she wanted him to give wasn't so certain any more. Yet he still wasn't speaking. She waited. Her breath held. Every second dragging before he finally cleared his throat and offered Caroline a reply.

'Sounds like a great idea,' he said.

46

This was good news, Holly told herself repeatedly as she sat up in bed, rehearsing what she was going to say to Giles over and over in her head. It was definitely a good thing. It would give them a chance to talk, to clear the air. She could say something about Rhubarb jumping on the computer and how she hadn't actually meant to send that email at all. It was just her thoughts while typing. Thoughts she wasn't even sure were true. And she could tell him about Sienna and the things she said while they were away, like the comment about persuading Giles not to have children. And while they were talking about the spa, she would reinforce how she had absolutely not demanded to do anything the entire weekend. All decisions had been made between the three of them. Yes, this journey would be good. It would give them a chance to talk properly and reconnect. That was what she kept telling herself.

As was now a common occurrence in Holly's bedtime routine, sleep evaded her. It felt like every half hour, she woke up, pulse racing as she checked the time, wondering whether she had slept in and Giles had gone without her. Whether she wanted him to or not, she couldn't decide.

By five thirty, she had given up altogether and was in the shower, deciding what she wanted to wear. Jeans and a T-shirt would've been her normal choice, but Caroline had already found this exhibition online and it really looked like a fancy affair. It was taking place in a remote hotel with a view of the sea and it was the type of event that served champagne and canapés even though you didn't have to buy tickets. If she didn't look good enough, they might not let her in and she could just imagine how much Sienna would love that.

So, once she was clean and dried, Holly spent almost an hour picking out an outfit.

Her eyes fell on a royal-blue dress with embroidered flowers that she had worn several years ago to some birthday party or another. She couldn't remember what the event was, but she remembered how Giles had looked at her in it, the corners of his mouth twisting into a smile. 'You look pretty decent in that,' he'd said. 'Pretty decent' – those were the words he'd used. Hardly the greatest compliment a man had ever given someone, and yet thinking about it now caused her stomach to flutter. Why would that happen? She'd probably just made some snarky comment back to him at the time. There certainly hadn't been any stomach fluttering.

She was being ridiculous, and she needed to get over it. Still, she picked up the blue dress and slipped it on anyway.

Feeling fairly confident about the choice, she checked the mirror, only to feel like something was wrong. She brushed down her dress, checking it was all straight, but even then, the outfit didn't feel right. The dress fit perfectly, and she was wearing the same silver studs she always wore. Just like she was wearing the same silver necklace and the same rings on her fingers. That was when it struck her. It was her engagement ring. It didn't feel right. Not with the outfit. Perhaps not with her any more, either.

Holly lifted her hand to stare at the ring. She wasn't engaged. She hadn't recently lost her almost-fiancé. And yet, here she was, walking around with a clear sign telling the world that she wasn't available to love anyone else. If she meant anything of what she said about wanting to move on then surely this had to be the very first step?

Her hands trembled as she slipped the ring over her knuckle and off her finger, her vision blurring with tears as she looked at it.

'You know this doesn't mean I love you any less, don't you?' she said, as if Evan was there, listening to her. Her heart throbbed as if it was breaking all over again. 'I will always love you with my whole heart. But I've got to stop living my life like time ended when you died. You understand, don't you?' She let out a brief chuckle that caused a stray tear to tumble down her cheeks. 'Of course you understand. You understood everything. I know I won't find someone who I love the way I love you. They don't exist. You know that, right? It's just not possible. I think that's maybe why I've been so scared to open my heart: because I knew no one could compare to you. But that's okay. They don't have to. I want to love again. Evan, I want someone to love me again.'

The tears were tumbling freely now, but she needed to get it all out. This was it. The only time she would do this, and she wanted to say everything right.

'This doesn't mean I'll forget what you did for me. As long as I live, I will never forget you. Thank you. Thank you for being the love of my life.'

Still wiping away the tears, Holly moved over to her dressing table. She still had the same small ring box Evan had been carrying all those years ago. The icy water had left it damaged, a

little like her. The catch no longer closed and the leather from
the top had peeled away, but it still served its purpose. Lifting the
ring to her lips, she kissed it gently once before placing it in
the box.

'Goodbye, my love,' she said.

Holly's heart somersaulted as she opened the front door. Obviously, she wasn't the only one who'd thought about making an impression. Giles had turned up in his racing green vintage sports car – the same car he had taken her out in for dinner on the first day they met all those years ago. Gosh, she had thought their relationship was complicated then, and it had been.

She'd actually thought she liked him, in a romantic sense. He, on the other hand, was just spending time with her because he was trying to get her business. No, that wasn't fair. He did like spending time with her. He just liked the idea of owning her business more. But now they were past that and were in an even bigger mess.

Giles didn't even look in her direction as Holly opened the car door and slipped inside. Instead, he was typing into the sat nav on his phone. When that was done, he sat back, switched on the engine and began to reverse out of the drive. All without a single word to her. So much for thinking they were going to clear the air.

It wasn't until they turned out of Bourton onto the Fosse Way road that he actually spoke.

'Why don't you use the time to get some sleep,' he said. 'And don't worry, I'll drive fast. I don't want this to take any longer than you do.'

Holly opened her mouth, then closed it again. The last thing she wanted was to get into an argument before they were even out of the Cotswolds. But then, if he wasn't going to speak to her, why the hell had he agreed to the trip?

The longer the silence endured, the more Holly's mind spiralled. Had he seen the email, or not? That was the first question she wanted to ask. The second was, had he spoken to Faye? Faye would completely back up Holly, at least with the pub situation, which would be enough to prove Sienna was a liar. Those two questions were the minimum she needed answers to, but this stony silence was making it impossible to know where to start, and when she did finally speak, over an hour and a half into the journey, it was a very different question that left her lips.

'I take it you didn't say anything to Sienna?' she asked.

Giles scoffed. 'No. Of course not.'

'Right. Of course you didn't say anything to her,' Holly said, struggling with the silence that was falling between them again. 'Why would you say anything? You love her. You're going to marry her.'

'Exactly.'

'That's why we're going to look at flowers.'

'Right. Because I love her.'

Holly nodded again. It was all the things that weren't being said that were painful. That felt as though they were physically pulling at every muscle in her body. She couldn't manage the rest of the car journey with this level of tension. She wouldn't survive. Her head would explode.

'I wrote you an email,' she said.

For the first time, Giles's eyes flicked off the road to look at her. 'I know.'

'Did you... did you read it? The other one, I mean, did you read...' She was about to ask if he'd read the one she'd asked him to delete when Giles slammed the steering wheel.

'Oh, for crying out loud,' he said.

Holly looked at the road in front of her. The traffic was less than ideal, with several lorries, et cetera, but she'd seen worse. That was until she looked at the sat nav and saw that the time of the journey had just gone up by an hour and a half. With four hours still to go, it was as if they had made no progress at all. Maybe Giles's first suggestion that she go to sleep to get through the trip wasn't such a bad idea after all.

48

Holly did sleep. Despite bouncing around in the sports car with no form of comfortable headrest, other than her jumper, she actually managed over two hours. Unfortunately, that still meant she had over two hours left until they reached their destination and another four back, but at least it was something.

'This is beautiful,' she said, as she looked out of the window. At some point, Giles had come off the motorway, and they were now driving down a tree-lined A-road. It was far flatter than she expected – a sign they probably weren't in Wales yet, but the fields were alive with the colours of late spring.

'Do you remember when we used to do this?' she said softly.

'Do what?'

'Just go for a drive. When I was pregnant with Hope, you'd just take me in the car to a hidden pub in some tiny village. Or sometimes, we wouldn't even do that. We'd just drive around for hours.'

'I remember,' Giles said. 'Those were the days when you were embarrassed to be seen with me.'

Her head snapped around to face him. 'I wasn't embarrassed to be seen with you.'

Although, as her eyes met his, she knew that wasn't true. For a split second, they just stared at one another before Giles's eyebrow rose, ever so slightly, and a smile twitched at the corners of his lips.

'Okay, maybe that's a little true,' she said. 'But you were pretty embarrassing back then.'

The conversation was a long way from flowing, but it was a lot better than it had been at the start of the trip and, as they continued, it was clear to Holly that both she and Giles were sticking to very neutral topics: the naming day, her parents' health, and how Hope was practising constantly for her upcoming spring concert. Yet, as they neared their destination, Holly could feel the questions burning in her throat. Things she would've had no problem asking had they not kissed.

'Where are Sienna's family?' she asked, broaching the subject as cautiously as possible. She couldn't come straight out and call her a liar without at least some type of preamble, could she?

'I'm not sure where all of Sienna's family is, to be honest,' Giles said. 'I know she's got a couple of relatives abroad. She was actually born in Singapore... or Bangkok, one of the two, so that makes sense.'

Holly bit down on her lip. She wasn't going to respond to it. She wasn't. But it was so difficult.

Giles looked across from the driver's seat. 'What is it?'

'No, it's nothing,' Holly said.

'That's obviously not true. It's obviously something, or you wouldn't be pulling that weird face.'

'I'm not pulling a weird face.'

'You absolutely are. I swear to God, if you don't tell me why you're sitting in my sports car looking constipated, I will stop right now and kick you out.'

Frustration shot through her, but Holly sighed a long sigh and relented.

'Do you not think that perhaps you should know a little bit more about Sienna before you marry her? I mean, you don't even know where her family is from. And six months, I mean, can anyone really know a person properly in six months? I don't think you can. You don't even live together yet.'

'You're saying I don't know Sienna?'

It was an outright question and a perfect opportunity to give an outright answer, but she couldn't do that.

'Have you spoken to Faye?' she said instead.

'Faye? What's Faye got to do with this?'

This was it. She had to get it out, or she'd go insane.

'I just wondered if you'd spoken to her. If she'd had anything to say about the weekend? You know. Like how I *demanded* we go to the pub and that type of thing.'

Holly could see the anger simmering away in Giles. This was not how the conversation was meant to go at all, but she didn't know how to get out of it. She was too far in now.

'She's sent me a couple of messages,' Giles said. 'She said she had a really lovely time and to thank Sienna for arranging it. That's what people normally do when a friend does something nice. They say thank you.'

She knew it was a dig, aimed at getting a rise out of her, but she didn't care. She ignored it. He hadn't answered her question.

'Can you just tell me if you've spoken to her?' She reached her hand across the gear stick and placed it on top of his. It was something she must've done dozens of times, and yet a sharp spark of electricity fired between the two of them. Hurriedly, she pulled her hand back.

'You have to understand, I just... I just don't want you to get hurt. You know that's all I care—'

She didn't have a chance to finish her sentence. The car suddenly swerved and Holly gasped as she grabbed the door handle. Before she could work out what was happening, they had stopped again; Giles had pulled the car up onto the verge where he slammed on the brakes and looked at her.

'You want to do this?' he said. 'Do you really want to do this now?'

49

The anger in his voice was enough to bring Holly to tears. She opened her mouth to speak, to explain herself, but even drawing breath was enough to make the tears flow faster.

Hastily, she wiped her face. Giles let out a loud groan.

'Let's just get through today, okay?' he said. 'Let's go to this damn exhibition so that I can find my fiancée the florist of her wedding dreams.'

His fiancée. It wasn't the first time on this journey that he'd said that. Actually, it felt like he said it more than Sienna's name. Was it to reinforce a point? They would be getting married, and anything Holly said about the woman would be seen as a personal slight on Giles? Or was it something else? He'd already said he'd seen her email, so was he responding without replying? Yes, now she thought about it, that felt like exactly what was happening.

Holly's tears were replaced with a numbness.

'Okay.' She nodded as her voice choked out the words. 'You're right. Let's just get through this.'

For the last remaining hour of the car journey, Holly didn't even attempt to speak. There was nothing she could say. At least, no questions she could ask that she would like to hear the answers to. And yet, as they drove upwards along a steep and winding track and reached a set of large, cast-iron gates, she couldn't help the words from slipping out of her mouth.

'Wow,' she said. 'It's a freaking castle.'

'It would appear so.'

'Imagine getting married here. Hope would absolutely love it.' Holly hadn't meant to mention weddings. It had just been an absent-minded comment. And yet Giles sniffed.

'Sienna wants a child-free venue,' he said.

Holly's eyes widened. 'Child-free?'

That wasn't something she'd expected. Obviously, Giles didn't have children of his own, but even if you didn't consider Hope or Jamie's kids, there were still his nephew and nieces, Faye's children. It seemed bizarre that he wouldn't want them there.

'What about what you want?'

'That's not really the focus of a wedding. It's the bride's day.'

'No, it's a day where you celebrate your love. It's a union. It's not a day where only one person gets what they want.'

'Well, making her happy is what I want, so I guess that's fine, isn't it?'

There was nothing Holly could say to that. Giles's eyes remained locked on the driveway ahead, as if he couldn't bear to look at her. Trying to ignore the weight building in her stomach, Holly did the only thing she could and stared out at the view, just like he was doing.

The building was the antithesis of the spa that Sienna had taken them to. This place was steeped in history, and for once, Holly found herself wishing she knew more about things like that, about architecture, or what kind of person would've loved this place. Hopefully, they had a bit of information inside she could read.

They were almost out of the car when a large man ran out from behind them.

'Parking is over towards the left!' a voice called out, although Holly was more intrigued by his vehicle than what he was saying.

'Is that a golf buggy?' Holly said. 'Is there a golf course here? I've not been in a golf buggy before. That shouldn't really be a surprise, should it, given that I don't play golf, but I just feel like I should've been in one somewhere.'

Giles shrugged. 'Probably. Are you going to ask questions constantly? I don't think I can cope with your babbling today.'

The comment hit her hard, stinging sharply before transforming into something different. Into anger. Holly had assumed Giles didn't know what the real Sienna was like. But what if he knew exactly what she was like, and that was what he wanted?

Following the man's instructions, they continued to drive around to the left of the castle, where they parked up. Holly didn't bother saying anything as she climbed out of the car, just like she didn't bother checking behind her to see if Giles was there as she followed the signs into the building. She needed to take photographs. Not speak to him. And like he said, the sooner they got this done, the sooner they could leave.

50

Holly was still smarting from Giles's comment. It was the harshness that had taken her by surprise. He knew she only ever babbled like that when she was nervous, and if that was the case, he was normally sweet about it. Usually, he made a joke to help ease her tension. But there was none of that today. It was just cruel, and it certainly hadn't helped her nerves.

Trying to swallow back the torrent of emotions filling her, Holly approached the mammoth set of doors marking the entrance to the hotel, though before they stepped inside, it became apparent why an event like this could keep the riff-raff out without being ticketed. (And ignoring the fact that it was miles from anywhere. For the last thirty minutes of the drive, they had barely seen a house. Let alone something that would constitute a town.) Two large doormen – or bouncers, she wasn't sure what the difference was – cut intimidating figures as they stood on the stone steps dressed in dark-green suits.

'We're here to see the flowers?' Holly said.

'The Leopold Garcia exhibition,' Giles said as he stepped in front of her. Holly scowled. Of course he could remember the name, but it wasn't like they wouldn't know what she was talking about.

'Of course. The exhibition is in the east wing of the building,' one bouncer said. 'There is a restaurant in the orangery in the west wing, but the rest of the hotel is reserved for overnight guests. This includes the smoking room and bar.'

'Good job neither of us smoke, then,' Holly said, instantly regretting her decision to speak. Why on earth had she thought now would be a good time to crack a joke? She didn't do jokes, and this moment proved why. It was obviously the nervousness. That was the problem. Apparently, when she couldn't get the babbling under control, she turned into a terrible stand-up comedian.

The bouncer nodded at Giles, ignoring Holly completely.

'Let's go in,' Giles said. He took one step forward, then turned to the bouncer. 'Where did you say the restaurant was?'

'Down the corridor, turn right.'

Holly didn't bother saying anything. Her stomach had been growling for the last forty-five minutes, and she definitely wanted something to eat too. Besides, it appeared she had to do whatever Giles said.

Holly had already expected that her friendship with Giles would change. There was nothing she could do about that. What she hadn't thought was that it would disappear altogether, but it looked like it was going to go that way. Fast.

51

If Holly had thought the awkward silence in the car journey was bad, it was nothing compared to the tension that surrounded them as they walked into the restaurant. With light streaming in through the tall windows, the phenomenal view out over the sea and the exposed brickwork crawling with ivy and passionfruit flowers, it was the type of place that would look romantic under any circumstances, but today, it seemed to be filled only with couples – all of them truly, madly in love.

'Let me guess – looking for wedding centrepieces?' the waitress asked as she placed the menus down in front of them. 'They're amazing. I keep finding myself tempted to pinch a couple. Didn't you find that?'

'We haven't actually been into the exhibition yet,' Holly said.

'No? Well, you're in for a treat. You'll love it. I tried to bring my fiancé to have a look at them too,' she said, flashing the ring on her finger. 'Not that we can afford any of it, mind. I just wanted to have a look, but he wouldn't come.' She looked at Holly and grinned. 'Guess you've got yours better trained than mine.'

'Oh, he's not mine. We're not together,' Holly said.

'Oh! I just thought you said—'

'Can we get a bottle of water, please?' Giles cut her off mid-sentence. 'Sparkling.'

The waitress's cheeks reddened. 'Of course. Yes, sorry. I'll get that for you now.'

As she scurried away, Holly glowered at Giles.

'Well, that was incredibly rude,' she said.

'She was waffling on, and we don't have time for that. It's already three o'clock. I doubt the traffic will be any better on the way home.'

'Remind me that next time I'm stuck on a long car journey with you, I need to take snacks. You're worse than Hope when you're hangry.'

Giles huffed, folding his arms, but a second later, he unfolded them again and stood up.

'What are you doing now?' Holly asked.

'I need to go to the bathroom. Is that okay? When did you become so damn nagging?'

Holly felt her annoyance mingle with guilt as Giles walked away. She'd been right to call him out for being rude, but then, he had been the one to drive all the way here with no breaks. He was probably tired as well as hungry. And she hadn't needed to question him about where he was going.

She glanced around the room but was surprised to find that Giles hadn't walked towards the bathroom door. Instead, he was standing at the bar next to the waitress he had snapped at. Holly tried to work out what they were talking about – they were definitely talking – but the restaurant was far too busy to hear anything and a moment later, Giles was walking away, towards the bathroom, while the waitress was coming towards Holly with a bottle of sparkling water.

'Thank you,' Holly said as she took the glass. 'Sorry, I don't mean to be nosy, but what did he just say to you? The man I'm with?'

'Oh, he just apologised, that's all. Said he'd had a bad couple of days and shouldn't have taken it out on me. Also, he said I could look forward to a nice tip to make up for it, and I wasn't to share it with the rest of the staff, as I was the only one he'd been rude to. To be honest, I've had people at this place say worse and not apologise, so... Anyway, I'll come back in a minute to take your order.'

'Thank you. Thank you very much.'

When Giles returned to the table, Holly didn't say anything about the waitress. It was difficult to know what to say. They couldn't possibly have moved to the stage in their friendship where they could only speak about the weather and the drive up, could they? Actually, speaking about the drive up would hardly be positive either, so that didn't leave much.

Holly cleared her throat, deciding it was probably a safe bet to talk about Jamie and the others, when she noticed how the restaurant seemed to be getting quieter. She looked around, wondering if there was some reason, like someone bringing a cake out for a birthday, or perhaps a person on their knee proposing, when a voice rose above everyone else.

'For crying out loud, is it really that difficult? Are you an idiot or something?'

52

Every person in the restaurant was looking in the same direction, and what had previously been a warm and inviting atmosphere was suddenly hushed and nervous. Only one voice could be heard.

'Did you hear what I said? I said, are you an idiot?'

The man was one of the few people not part of a couple, but with a small group of other men. They all appeared to be a similar age: early forties perhaps. His accent was from London, and though Holly couldn't be sure, there was something about the way his words ran into one another that made her think he'd been drinking. The person he was speaking to was the waitress who had served them. The same waitress Giles had got annoyed with because she was continually talking. But she wasn't now. Right now, she was standing where she was, shoulders back, as she fought, but failed, to stop her bottom lip from trembling.

'I—'

'Idiot? Did you hear what I said?' The rest of his table chuckled, as if he had said the funniest thing in the world, while the rest of the restaurant remained deadly silent.

The waitress cleared her throat again, but no words came out.

Holly was too stunned to move. It was horrid enough seeing something like this anywhere, but in such a beautiful location full of people trying to enjoy some special time together, the man's behaviour was absolutely disgusting.

'That poor girl,' Holly whispered. 'Whatever has happened, she doesn't deserve to be spoken to like that.'

'No,' Giles muttered. 'She doesn't.'

'You know, this is ridiculous,' the man continued. 'A place like this should have far better staff. You know how much money we pay? You know that our meal probably costs more than you earn in a month?'

He really was vile. The worst kind of human, and every word he spoke made Holly sick to her stomach. She could only imagine how the waitress felt.

'Get the kitchen to sort it. Or we'll get you sacked. That's a promise.'

Holly looked back across the table towards Giles, ready to ask if she should do something, but he was already pushing the chair back and standing.

'Giles?' Holly said, but he didn't respond. He was too busy marching across the restaurant towards the man.

53

Holly didn't know what to do. She was sure there were plenty of people in the hotel who could deal with the man. There was probably even somebody coming to sort it now. But Giles was already halfway across to their table. If she tried to stop him, she would just make the scene even bigger, and it would probably take even longer for everybody to get back to enjoying their meal. She just had to trust that he knew what he was doing.

'Thank you, Clara,' Giles said, tapping the waitress lightly on the shoulder. 'I'll take it from here.'

The waitress looked at him but seemed unable to respond. Instead, her mouth simply hung open.

'I said, I can take it from here,' he repeated.

She nodded rapidly and hurried away, out through the back of the bar. Hopefully, Holly thought, to find somebody in management before the situation escalated any further. But for all the anger she knew he felt, Giles was looking incredibly calm.

'So, what appears to be the problem?' He spoke in his best English accent, that smooth Mr Darcy tone Holly had seen hundreds of women melt to before. But he wasn't dealing with women. He was dealing with men – drunk, cross men.

The man frowned. 'What are you – the manager? I'll tell you what happened. She gave me the bloody weekend menu. That's what she did. Then when I tried to order stuff, she said I couldn't have it. Stupid, just like I said.'

Giles tilted his head to the side slightly, as if absorbing all the information he had just been given.

'So you verbally attacked a person for making a genuine mistake?'

'It's her job!'

'Yes, yes, you're right. And I'm sure you have never made a genuine mistake in your job. I'm sure you are perfect at everything you do.'

The man coughed and cleared his throat slightly. 'I just wanted to enjoy my meal.'

'Isn't that a coincidence,' Giles said, 'because that's exactly why I came in here – to enjoy a meal.'

'Hang on. I thought you said you were the manager.'

'No, no, you just assumed that. A mistake, I guess you'd say? Or stupidity? I'm not sure.'

The man's cheeks flushed red, and Holly's heart jolted up into her throat.

'Are you saying I'm stupid?' The man's face turned puce. 'I'll show you—'

He went to stand, but Giles grabbed him at the top of the shoulder, right on the inside of his collarbone.

'Oh no,' Giles said. 'You don't want to go there.' In an instant, his demeanour changed. His eyes narrowed, and the tension in the room felt a hundred times higher than it had before. For Holly, at least, and that was saying something. Her whole body was on tenterhooks, waiting to see what happened. It didn't look like a particularly aggressive movement on Giles's part, but from the way the man was wincing, Holly assumed Giles knew exactly what he was doing.

For the first time, one of the other men at the table spoke. 'Craig, maybe we should—'

'No,' Craig said. 'I'm not gonna be intimidated by somebody like him. Stupid snob.'

'Snob?' Giles once again tilted his head. 'Quite possibly. Stupid? Absolutely not. Being stupid would be you thinking there is any way of you getting out of this situation with what you want. The best-case scenario is you get up now and you leave, and because I'm feeling generous, if you leave right now, I will pay for the excessive number of drinks you've already had. Any tab you've got open, I will cover. That's how much I want you out of this room, so that I can enjoy my meal. But if you don't want to go... well, I'd rather that didn't happen, because I've been having a rough couple of weeks lately, and that would just make it worse. But it's your prerogative. You can insist on staying, in which case, we will all have to wait here until the police come, and all these good people watching will give their statements as to how you physically attacked me when I came over to this table, ever so politely, and asked you to quieten your noise.'

'What? I didn't do that?'

'Really?' Giles looked at a random table. 'You saw him, right?'

'Absolutely. Yes, absolutely,' a woman replied. Several other people hurriedly nodded.

Without even a hint of a smirk at having got people so quickly onside, Giles turned back to Craig. 'They will all give their statements, and I might even press charges. So you have a choice – leave content that you've already enjoyed a load of free drinks, or stay and get a free night's accommodation in a police cell. I'm fine with either option.'

54

A genuine round of applause rose through the air the minute the men left the restaurant. By that time, the actual hotel manager had appeared and was looking most confused as the group scurried away, shame-faced. By contrast, Giles strolled back to his and Holly's table, receiving countless pats on the back en route.

'Thank you so much,' Clara, the waitress said when she came over to them. 'They were going to be trouble. They had the champagne brunch this morning and saw the free flow as a challenge. I said I didn't want them in, but it's not my job to make calls on something like that.'

'I'm just glad it's all sorted,' Giles said, 'and obviously I will pay for all of their drinks.'

'That's okay,' the waitress replied. 'Someone else covered it. They didn't want me to point out who, but they said that you'd already done your bit, they could do theirs. And somebody else paid for your meal too.'

'Really? Thank you. I... Thank you.'

She smiled broadly, clearly pleased at the effect their

generosity had had on Giles. 'I'll just go get your food. It shouldn't be a minute.'

A moment later, she was gone and the rest of the diners were getting back to the meals.

'Wow, quite the hero, aren't you?' Holly said, but she couldn't help grinning. 'Although you know, I'm not sure you'd have actually got away with lying to the police and saying he attacked you. They would have probably wanted to see some evidence of that.'

'I knew it would never get that far. I've dealt with hundreds of idiots like him on the yacht. People who think they're entitled to everything and that every person wearing a uniform is below them. The minute you actually call them out for their behaviour, they haven't got a leg to stand on.'

'Well, you did a good thing there. A really good thing.'

Rather than smiling at Holly's comment as she expected, Giles looked unusually saddened.

'You know, when I sometimes think about myself and how I spent so many years like Craig, thinking I was above people, it makes my skin crawl. I actually feel physically sick.'

'You were never that bad,' Holly said.

'I wasn't, but I was very close,' he replied. 'And then I do something like snap at a waitress, who's just being friendly like she's supposed to be, and it feels like I'm right back there again. Like I haven't changed. Like maybe this other version of myself has just been a facade.'

All the joy that had been buzzing around only a moment before was fading. Holly leaned across the table, needing to be closer so he knew she was listening.

'Giles, I have never known anybody who makes more of an effort to be a good person. Or doubts that they are so much. Everybody has bad days. Everybody has moments where they say things they regret. When they snap because they're tired or... in your case, hungry. That doesn't make you a bad person. And the fact that you're even thinking it does is proof of that.'

He nodded, but his gaze stayed fixed on the table. When Holly followed suit and looked down, she realised why. At some point, their fingers had become completely entwined. They crossed so perfectly and were so at ease, she hadn't even noticed. A thick lump filled her throat as her pulse began to rise.

'Right. Who ordered the fish?'

Holly looked up to see the waitress had returned with two plates. Hurriedly, she pulled her hands back and placed them on her lap.

'Look at that,' she said, avoiding Giles's gaze completely. 'Our food's come.'

55

The food was delicious, although due to the complimentary desserts they were given, they spent far more time eating than expected and it was almost four before they finally went to check out the flowers.

Holly wasn't sure what she had expected from a flower exhibition – probably vases. Beautiful vases filled with all different shapes, sizes and colours of blooms. But as she stepped into the first room, she felt the air rush from her lungs.

'How the hell did they get that in here?' she said.

Holly was looking at a structure that was at least ten feet high. The copper metal frame looked inches from the vaulted ceiling, and its tarnished orange blended perfectly with the reds and burnt umbers of the flowers cascading down from it. Suddenly, the word 'exhibition' made sense. She wasn't looking at wedding bouquets. She was looking at art.

'Okay, we are definitely not having anything like that,' Giles said.

'It's amazing.'

'No, not that one. That one.'

Holly followed his gaze to the other side of the room, where two large thrones had been built entirely out of foliage. There had to be some sort of structure beneath them, Holly thought. Something to stop them from losing their shape. Though even if they were sturdy, how would you sit on them? Surely you'd get grass stains on your clothes. Not to mention stains from all the flowers too. As certain as she was, she still felt the need to check with Giles.

'They're just for decoration, right?' she said. 'People don't actually sit on them, do they?'

'Oh, you can guarantee someone will try,' Giles replied.

As they continued to study the piece from a distance, a couple approached the thrones, nodding towards one another as they pointed.

'I think they might get one,' Holly whispered to Giles. 'Go on, I think you should ask to sit on it. You know, get a proper feel.'

'You just want to get us kicked out of here.' Giles chuckled. 'No, there's no way I'm having one of those things.'

'Well, whatever makes Sienna happy, makes you happy, so maybe she'll decide she must have them and you won't have a choice?' Holly smirked before taking out her phone. 'Come on, we need to get photos – that's why we're here.'

Whether every piece was to Holly's taste or not didn't change the fact that every piece was truly phenomenal. The way the artist used the flowers to create colours and textures was absolutely mesmerising, and Holly took photos of them all, although not once did she see anything that looked remotely like a bouquet. There were several arches, though, which she could easily see as places to say your vows beneath.

'I probably shouldn't show Hope any photos of this,' Holly said. 'She'll start pulling up Mum's flowers and trying to make her own creations.'

'And why shouldn't she?' Giles said. 'You never know – maybe it's her calling to be a flower sculptor, and she'll never know because you didn't allow her to try. Really, suppressing your daughter's natural talent? I expected more from you, Holly.'

'Okay, well, how about she tries in your house then? See how you like it?'

'Fine, you're on. When we get back, I'm taking her out for the day, and we are doing nothing but flower sculpting.'

'Oh, that I would absolutely love to see.'

As she rolled her eyes, Holly noticed a sign directing them outside.

'Come on,' she said. 'I heard someone saying that all the biggest sculptures are outside. I can't wait to see what those look like.'

56

'Oh wow, now this is amazing! Come on, Giles. Why are you so slow?' Holly practically sprinted out onto the grounds. It was beautiful. Such a stunning setting, with rough rock faces sloping down to the rolling waves of the sea. The lush lawns were covered in such soft, green grass, Holly could only imagine the fun Hope would have performing cartwheel after cartwheel. But it wasn't the grass or the sea that held her attention the most.

'Is that a giant rabbit?' she said, still racing towards a sculpture. 'Oh my God, this is amazing. This is my favourite. Jamie and I are getting one of these for the garden. I don't care what it costs. I need it.'

'You'd want a giant rabbit?' Giles's lips were tight, his expression almost scathing. For a second, Holly feared he was about to say something cutting and mean, like he'd done in the car, but then a wide slanted grin spread across his face. 'Would you really choose a giant rabbit when you could have a giant polar bear instead?'

'What?' Holly said, still grinning. Giles pointed behind her.

The creature was immense – at least twelve feet high and

covered in more white flowers than Holly had ever known existed.

'There's an otter over there too.'

'No, it's the polar bear. We need a polar bear. Come on, I want us to get a selfie underneath it.'

'Are you serious?'

'There's no way anyone will believe I saw a twelve-foot polar bear made out of flowers unless we have a photo under it. Now hurry up!'

She turned to move towards the polar bear, only for a loud horn to stop her in her tracks. It only took her a moment to realise where the sound had come from.

One of the golf buggies was cutting its way through the exhibition. From the way they were zigzagging, it didn't look like something they were supposed to be doing.

'Get out of the way, suckers!'

Holly recognised the voice before she saw the face driving. It was the same man from the restaurant – the one who had caused a complete scene. They were currently performing loops around various sculptures, scattering people, who ran screaming. Behind them, another golf buggy was in pursuit.

'Ladies and gentlemen,' a man was calling from the back of the second buggy. 'We are sorry about the disturbance. The police have been called. Please go inside until the situation is under control.'

The first golf buggy was veering away from them now, towards the edge of the manor. Holly couldn't move as she watched it. What the hell was wrong with people? They could kill someone in that thing. Somebody's life could be entirely ruined because of some idiot deciding to do something reckless. It wasn't only their own life they were playing with. It was innocent people's lives too. And these weren't children messing around. These were adults.

'Holly? Holly, we need to go inside,' Giles said. 'Actually, maybe we should use this as a sign to get going. We don't want to get caught up in the police turning up and everything. At that rate, we'll never get home.'

Holly nodded; that made sense. There were plenty of witnesses around. She was sure she and Giles wouldn't be able to add anything more to the situation and this was not something he could talk down. The police were needed.

'Okay,' she said, only to hesitate. 'Can we just get a selfie with that polar bear first?'

Giles looked in the direction the buggy had gone. There didn't seem to be any sign of it coming back.

'Sure, come on.'

Together, they quickly darted over towards the giant polar bear, and Holly grabbed her phone out of her pocket.

'My arms are longer – give it to me,' Giles said. 'Besides, you know I take better pictures.'

'You don't,' Holly said, 'but you do have longer arms, so I'll give you that.'

He stretched his arm out, then pointed the camera towards them and angled it so that the polar bear – or as much of it as they could fit – was in the shot too.

'Okay, we're going to need to get closer to get the whole thing in.'

In what seemed like the most normal, natural motion, Giles placed his arm around Holly's waist and pulled her into his side. But her body's reaction was anything but normal. It felt like every fibre of her being had been set alight with static shocks. Tingles spread out from where he touched her, all the way to her chest, causing her pulse to rocket. And when she lifted her head up, she found she wasn't facing the camera any more. In fact, Giles was no longer holding the camera up; it was down by his side. Both their bodies had somehow twisted around, so their chests were pressing together and her eyes were looking up into his. She didn't know how it had happened. It was like her body simply *needed* to be in this position. And maybe his did too.

'Holly,' Giles whispered. 'I don't know...'

He couldn't finish his sentence, but he didn't need to. Holly understood everything he was trying to say. Everything he felt – or at least she thought she did. This was it. This was the moment she had been waiting for. The moment she had to put it all on the line.

'Giles, what I wrote... We need to—'

A sudden crashing sound stole the words from her mouth and sent every nearby bird into the air.

'What the hell was that?' she said instead.

57

Holly didn't move. She wasn't sure if she could. Her entire chest was continuing to pound, although she didn't know whether that was to do with the closeness she and Giles had just shared, or the loud bang that had sent every bird fleeing. Either way, her hands were trembling.

'Giles, what do you think that was?'

His face had darkened. 'Honestly? I think they crashed the golf buggy.'

'What?' Holly looked in the direction she had seen the buggies disappear. 'Do you think they're okay? We need to go check.'

She moved to follow the rest of the crowd, who had now changed direction and, rather than heading back into the building as they had been requested to do, were scurrying around the side of it. But as she took a step, Giles grabbed her hand and pulled her back to him.

'Holly, I don't think that's a good idea.'

'They might be hurt. They might need help.'

'I know, which is—'

'Then they might need someone with first-aid training,' she said. 'It doesn't matter how horrible they are – I can't not help. And I might not be a doctor, but I've still done a lot of training. What was the point of all of that if I'm not going to help someone when they actually need it? Now, are you coming or not?'

All her questions were rhetorical. With a shake of her hand, she freed herself from Giles's grip before racing away from him and towards the source of the bang.

A thousand thoughts whirred through her head as she ran, trying to remember everything she'd learned from all those first-aid courses she had taken. Every year, she did the refreshers, and she had put various skills to use. Only last summer, she'd cleaned and bandaged the wound of a small child who had slipped in the river and cut their leg. She had also been moments away from using the village defibrillator when a customer at the bakery suffered a suspected heart attack – only someone had managed to grab a local doctor before she was required to put her skills to the test. But she had surprised herself with her calmness in those moments. The measured way in which her mind had slowed. She'd assessed the situation, knew what she needed to do. It would be the same here; she was sure of it. There had been no screaming. Was that good or not? She probably wouldn't know until she saw them.

'Holly, wait. Wait for me.'

As she turned the corner of the building, Giles was right by her side. He slipped his hand in hers, but she knew it wasn't to slow her down this time. It was just to make sure he stayed with her.

'Excuse me.' Holly raised her voice to the large crowd that had gathered. 'I need to get past. I need to get through.'

'People! Move!' Giles added.

Finally, they pushed their way through to the front of the

group and to the source of the commotion. It was indeed the drunk men from earlier, and they had indeed crashed the buggy, but they were all standing behind the vehicle and none of them seemed to have a drop of blood on them.

One, however, was crying while muttering, 'My wife is going to kill me. She's going to kill me.'

Holly stepped forwards and was still trying to work out what exactly had happened when Giles spoke.

'You have to be joking,' he said. 'You have got to be joking.'

58

Giles marched past Holly and everyone else until he was standing at the front of the golf buggy. The front of the golf buggy that was exactly where Giles's vintage car's wing mirror had been only minutes before. All down the side was a long scratch.

'It was the brakes,' Craig said. 'The brakes on these things don't work properly. This is the hotel's fault for having vehicles with dodgy brakes. This isn't our fault.'

'Please shut up, Craig,' one of the friends said.

'It's the gravel. It's—'

'Craig!' This time, it was all three of his friends simultaneously. Finally, Craig turned around as if he was about to pick a fight with one of his friends, but Holly didn't care what he was doing at all. What she cared about, or rather who, was Giles.

Giles had had this car for over a decade. Probably for over half his life. And as silly as it might be for some people to attach sentimental value to pieces of metal, she knew how many journeys he had been on with it, the places it had taken him. She herself was sentimentally attached to the car, so she couldn't imagine what it was like for him.

'Are you okay?' she asked.

For a second, he continued to stare, but he didn't move.

'We can't drive it like this,' he said. 'Legally. Not with a wing mirror like that. No, this needs to be fixed. Immediately.'

'Yes, yes, of course it does.' A woman wearing a tag with the word *Manager* written beneath her name, Evelyn, bustled her way next to Giles and Holly. 'I assume this is your vehicle,' she said. 'I'm ever so sorry. We know several great mechanics in the area. I'll get on the phone now. It'll be sorted, absolutely sorted. And obviously, we will pay for all the repairs. A complete repaint. Anything it needs.'

'Just get it good enough that I can drive it home,' Giles said. 'I'll let my mechanic deal with it there.'

'If that's what you want,' she said, 'and please, sit yourself in the smoking-room bar. Whatever you want, it's on the house. I'll just be a minute.'

Holly smiled gratefully at the woman, although she didn't know what to say. It wasn't her place to speak and Giles didn't look like he was in a place to say anything. Instead, he was crouching down by the car door, running his hand along the scratches as he inspected the damage.

'It was all original paintwork,' he said after a few minutes. 'This entire thing was original. It's not just the money; it's the history, you know?'

Holly wasn't sure if he was asking her, or if the question was rhetorical, but she replied anyway.

'I get it. I'm really sorry. I know how much it means to you, but it can be fixed. It might not be the same, but it can be fixed and you can still make more memories together.'

Holly wasn't sure what effect she expected her words to have, but immediately Giles stood up and nodded. 'You're right. I'm sorry. I shouldn't make a fuss. It's just a car. Just bits of metal and rubber.'

'Bits of metal and rubber that have meaning to you. That's okay.'

As their eyes locked, Giles let out a slight laugh and Holly was sure he was going to say something more, but a sudden thought struck her.

'You'd better ring Sienna. Tell her you're going to be late. Ben's staying with Hope so it's not a problem for me. But I'm sure she'll want to know where you are.'

As he shook his head, Giles let out a long groan that turned into a bitter chuckle.

'You know I bet she'll be happy about this. I suggested we use this car to take her to the wedding, or at least leave in it, but she dismissed that idea straight away. Apparently, she'd already got a theme in mind and this didn't fit with it.'

'Really?' Holly said. 'It's perfect.'

He shrugged. 'Her wedding, her choice.'

She could hear it in his voice. The defeatedness. Like he didn't have a say in his own future any more, and she needed to tell him he was wrong. He did have a choice. It was standing right there in front of him. But she couldn't say it Not now. Now he had enough on his mind.

59

While Giles took out his phone to call Sienna, Holly walked back into the building, where the doorman immediately directed her towards the smoking room; obviously, Evelyn had told them which people to look out for.

It was the type of room Holly could imagine loving most in winter. The grey stone walls were decorated with vibrant, modern paintings, while a large fireplace was currently unlit, but piled high with logs, ready for when the weather turned. Most of the space was filled with comfy-looking armchairs and sofas, around half of which were currently occupied. Though, rather than taking a seat, Holly headed over to the bar where a young barman was polishing glasses. For a second, she thought about choosing something sensible, like a lemonade or an orange juice, but even when they got the car done, she wasn't going to be the one driving it, and right now, after the day she'd had, she felt like she needed something stronger.

'Large glass of white wine,' she said.

'Sure, any preference? We've got a fantastic English supplier. They do some incredible whites.'

Holly didn't doubt the local wines were probably three times the price of the imported ones, but then again, Evelyn had already said that everything would be on the house.

'That's perfect,' she said, 'thank you.'

A minute later, a chilled glass of white was placed on the bar in front of her, and she took a long sip, only for a flood of memories to hit her. She had been wine-tasting once before, at a vineyard in France with Evan. It was the first time she'd ever been on a moped, the first time she'd ever been to a vineyard, the first time she'd considered that maybe Evan could be more than just a friend of Fin's.

After that, she had fallen pretty hard for him, although she'd tried her hardest not to. And there had been sensible reasons not to fall in love with him.

There had been the distance between where they lived, the fact that she had a daughter, and in terms of socio-economic status, they were a million miles apart. There had also been Giles too. She had thought he was out of her life, but then he had appeared on a boat and professed to still love her. But she had chosen Evan. That had been the right choice. For years and years, she had known that had been the right choice. And given the chance again, she wouldn't do it differently. But when she thought back on that moment, thought back to the words he'd said...

'Well, Sienna's fine with it.' Giles walked into the bar and sat down next to her. 'Diet Coke, please,' he said, before turning back to Holly. 'She's out and isn't going to be back tonight, so it doesn't matter to her. To be honest, she seemed to find the whole thing quite amusing. She liked the idea of golf buggies most of all.'

'I'm sure someone at home will be able to fix it properly,'

Holly replied, knowing that what Giles needed right now was a little optimism. 'Is it going to take a lot to make it drivable?'

Giles shook his head. 'I don't think so. The wing mirror has to be fixed and I want someone to give it a once-over first. It wouldn't be a responsible thing to drive unless someone's checked it.'

'Giles, always the responsible one.'

'Hey, you know I'm always responsible when it comes to my cars.'

'You're right,' Holly said. 'You are. Remember that time you helped Mum and I out of a ditch?'

'Hard to forget, really,' he said. 'You were a damsel in distress.'

'I was not a damsel in distress. Not at all. My mother was a damsel in distress. I was the sidekick.'

'Keep telling yourself that,' Giles said, a slightly slanted grin forming on his lips. Her stomach flipped at the sight of it. It was just good to see that grin again. 'So, already on the hard stuff?' Giles said, nodding to the glass of wine.

'Well, I thought if I had a couple, I might fall asleep on the drive back, and then you wouldn't have to talk to me.'

'That sounds perfect,' he said with a grin. 'I think I might need a sip, though.' He reached out his hand and Holly pushed the glass towards him. A moment later, he took a small mouthful.

'That's a good wine,' he said.

'I know.' She drew in a deep breath. They had said a lot of things today. Some of them hurtful, some of them a little thoughtless. But there were things she still needed to say and given how his day had already taken a sudden plummet, it felt like there was no time like the present. When she took the glass back, she took a long draw from it and put it back down. 'Giles, there's something I want to talk to you about—'

'Oh good, you found the bar.'

Holly turned her head to the doorway where Evelyn was standing. She strode towards them, a smile fixed on her face, although Holly couldn't help but feel that it looked a little unnatural. Like she was struggling to keep it there.

'So, I've got a couple of pieces of news,' she said.

'Great. You've found a mechanic, I take it,' Giles said.

'We have... but I'm afraid it's not great news. I've rung around all the local places, and unfortunately there is no one who can look at the car until morning.'

60

For a second, silence surrounded them. Several couples were talking quietly as they sipped on their drinks while a soft tinkling sound came from behind the bar, as the barman tidied and polished the wineglasses. But around the three of them – Evelyn, Holly and Giles – it was utterly silent.

Holly wasn't good at silence, and her instinct was to start filling it, but she couldn't be the first one to speak in this situation. After all, Evelyn hadn't spoken to her. And so, the pair of women looked at Giles and waited.

'I'm sorry,' he said eventually. 'You're saying you can't get a mechanic to come out until tomorrow?'

'It's five-fifteen,' she said. 'They've all closed up shop.'

'What about an emergency out-of-hours one?'

'I tried to find one, but they all said the same thing.'

'Which was?'

'As the car is currently in place where it is not a risk to anybody, it would be better just to leave it until the morning.'

Giles's jaw was rolling from side to side. Holly could see the anger burning within him. Leaning forward, she placed a hand on his arm.

'Okay,' she said. 'We can't get anyone to look at the car tonight, so what options do we have? Taxis? Can we get a taxi back to a train station?'

'There is a train station, but it's about a fifteen-mile drive away. Of course, if that's what you decide, we will sort a taxi there immediately. And we would refund all costs to get you home.'

Giles shook his head. 'That's a ridiculous idea. It's probably a five-hour train journey at least. We wouldn't get home until after midnight, at which point, I'd have to turn around again and spend the entire day coming back here so I could drive the car back again.'

Worded like that, it did sound like a ridiculous idea.

Evelyn coughed slightly, clearing her throat. Holly felt incredibly sorry for the woman. After all, none of this was her fault.

'Of course, I am aware of that, which is why I would like to offer you a room here. Everything complimentary, obviously. We have one mechanic who assured me they will be able to get here by 9 a.m. at the very latest.' She paused a moment before she continued. 'And obviously, the bar would be complimentary all night.'

Holly didn't reply. She couldn't. It wasn't up to her. An open bar and a stay in a luxury hotel felt ideal. After all, Hope was already spending the night at Ben's, so it wasn't like she'd have to rearrange anything there. It would also give her the chance she needed to finally tell Giles about Sienna. Not to mention have an actual discussion about the email she'd sent him. But it wasn't her decision to make. She looked at Giles.

'Whatever you want to do,' she said. 'It's up to you. Do you want to stay?'

Finally, he let out a long, drawn-out sigh.

'Fine,' he said. 'But we're having the best rooms in the house.'

61

'I'll have a glass of whatever she's got,' Giles said before changing his mind. 'Scrap that. We're here all night. We'll have the bottle. And we'll probably need another one later, so make sure they're chilled.'

He muttered a quiet thank you as the barman placed the bottle in front of him, then he topped up Holly's glass and filled his own to the brim without another word.

'You know, some days, you think things can't get any worse, and then something like *this* happens,' he said after a long gulp.

The words stung.

'Today hasn't been all bad,' she said. 'Looking at the flowers was great. And lunch was lovely, after you kicked out Craig.'

'You're right,' he sighed. 'It's just... you know. It is what it is, right?'

Holly wasn't sure if she knew what he meant after all. Sure, the car journey had been pretty horrific, but was he talking about spending time with her *full stop*? Is that where the problem had been?

'At least this wine is good.' He took another drink, and Holly's eyes widened as she realised he had already polished off his entire glass in a matter of minutes. Giles was always a very sensible drinker. Often he was the designated driver in the group. This wasn't like him at all. Yet he immediately poured himself another glass.

'I know you don't want to do this—' Holly started.

'You're right, I don't. I *don't* want to do this.' He turned and looked her in the eye. There was so much pain there. So much guilt. She could see it now – however hard this had been for her, it had to be ten times harder for him. After all, *he* was the one who was engaged. Only he was engaged to a woman who wasn't right for him on any level. She was a liar. She was manipulative, and she was going to force him into a future he didn't want to live. This wasn't about her. It was about them.

'Giles, there are things I *need* to talk to you about,' she said.

'No. No, you don't, Holly.' He turned back away from her. 'We don't need to talk. We don't have to, and I don't want to.'

'Please, if you could just listen—'

His head snapped back around, and this time, when he looked her in the eye, she could see nothing but anger.

'Okay, let me put it out there as clear as I can. If I could go back and change the past, I would do so in a heartbeat. But I can't, and now I have to live with that. That's all there is to it.'

'Wow.' With the single word, Holly was left breathless. He was right. He had made it perfectly clear. If he could go back and change what had happened between them, he would. At least she knew where she stood now. 'Okay, I guess you're right. I guess there's nothing to talk about.'

It was her turn to down her glass of wine. As she did, she turned her head away from him so he couldn't see the tears in her eyes. She had made a couple of bad decisions in the past. Things that people would definitely call mistakes. But did she ever wish she could go back and undo them? Other than that winter's walk by the lake, she couldn't think of one thing she would simply erase from her life.

She emptied her glass and reached for the bottle – at the exact same time as Giles. When their hands touched, she hastily pulled hers away, and in one sweeping move, wiped the tears from her cheeks.

'Holly, you have to understand what I meant is—'

'I get it. It's fine.'

'No, no—'

'Okay, the room is all sorted if you'd like me to show you up to it,' Evelyn interrupted. 'I have to say, you've lucked out a little bit. We're almost fully booked, and the only room available is our honeymoon suite. So I guess that's a bit of a silver lining, isn't it?'

Giles and Holly exchanged identical stunned looks.

'I'm sorry,' Holly said, still sniffing back any remaining tears. 'Did you just say the honeymoon suite?'

'Yes,' Evelyn said brightly. 'We do lots of weddings here. It's where the bride and groom stay.'

'We understand what a honeymoon is,' Giles said, 'but it was the singular "suite" that we didn't understand. You're saying there's only one room?'

'Yes, it's the only one left in the hotel. Like I said, we're almost fully booked. That won't be a problem, will it?'

62

On the top floor of the hotel, Evelyn was still hoping to win them over with her broad smile, which was flickering more and more with every passing second. 'It's a super king bed,' she said. 'I actually have one of these at home and there's room for me, my wife, the two kids and the dog. Actually, if it's just my wife and me in there, it sometimes feels like we're sleeping in a different bed. She's that far away from me.' She let out a strained laugh before she continued. 'The fridge is fully stocked, and obviously everything is complimentary. And it's up to you if you want to eat in the restaurant or get room service. You won't be charged a penny, I promise. Now, I shall leave you to it. Of course, the option for a taxi to the train station is still there if you want it. Just let me know. Preferably before seven thirty. That's when I clock off.'

'Thank you,' Holly said.

A moment later, the door closed, and she and Giles were alone together in the room.

'I'm going to check out the bathroom,' Holly said. Despite the size of the suite, it suddenly felt incredibly cramped. 'You know. After the drive and everything.'

They still hadn't brought up the issue of the one bed, but she was planning on putting that off for as long as possible.

'I guess it's through there,' Giles said, pointing to a wooden door.

Without another word, Holly stepped into the adjoining room, only to let out a small gasp.

'Is that a roll-top and a Jacuzzi bath? In one?'

'It does appear to be,' Giles said as he sidled up beside her. 'If I'd known they did something like that, I'd have put one in the cottage for you.'

'I don't think we could've fitted one of those in the cottage,' Holly replied, although as she spoke, another thought struck her. 'I know I never really thanked you enough for that,' she said. 'For the cottage.'

'No, that's because you were too busy being mad at me for going behind your back,' Giles muttered.

'You're right, I was. I still am. I don't like you going behind my back, but that time in my life was so much easier because of what you did for me. Actually, several times in my life have been so much easier because of the things you've done for me. I appreciate that. I just want you to know that I do.'

'I do,' he said.

'And I'm sorry about the email.'

'Holly, I—'

'I'm sorry. I wasn't thinking straight. I shouldn't have sent it. I didn't send it, actually. I mean I did but...'

She was moving towards him again. She wanted to be able to see into his eyes and for him to see into hers. She wanted him to know that she was telling the truth.

'I'd never do anything to mess up our friendship, Giles. You are the most important—'

'Don't. Don't do it.' Giles lifted his hand into the air. He shook his head. 'Why don't you run yourself a bath,' he said. 'I've got some emails I need to send anyway.'

Holly opened her mouth, only to close it again. There was nothing else to say right now. 'Okay, yes, okay.'

Given how phenomenal the bath was, it should have been the most relaxing of Holly's life. The Jacuzzi jets were strategically placed for a perfect massage, and an array of luxury lotions and potions filled ceramic jars all within perfect reach of where she lay in the perfectly hot water. And yet, she couldn't relax. Not with Giles just there on the other side of the door, refusing to hear her out. Refusing to even listen to her or let her explain. She had made a mistake, and she wanted to apologise and explain. Was that really the worst thing in the world? If he was a friend, shouldn't he let her explain?

He was being selfish. He was putting this all on her, and it wasn't all on her. She might not have remembered the exact moment of the kiss, but she actually felt like maybe none of it had been on her at all. Who was to say he wasn't the one who had kissed her first? She was absolutely the person who broke away. If she hadn't stopped kissing him, who knows what might have happened? And yet he was there, making her feel guilty. She wasn't going to have it any more. She wasn't.

She jumped out of the bath, splashing water on the floor as she reached out and grabbed one of the towelling robes. It really was a phenomenally soft robe, and under normal circumstances, she'd probably look to see where it had come from, but her mind was too focused right now. She and Giles were having this out. Perhaps this situation, them being stuck in the hotel together, was some perverse way of fate trying to make them have the conversation. She might not know that for sure, but what she did know was that they weren't going to get a chance like this again, and she wasn't going to let it slip by.

Still tying a knot in her robe, and with the end of her hair dripping around her shoulders, she marched into the living room, where Giles was still typing on his phone.

'I'm not all to blame for this,' she said.

'Sorry?'

'Don't "sorry" me, you know what I'm talking about. This. What happened between us.'

'Holly, please don't do this.' He stood up and walked towards her.

'Can you not at least respond? I told you I loved you. I put my heart on the line, and you're just going to be angry with me? Or worse still, ignore me?'

Finally, Giles put his phone down and looked at her. 'You really want to do this?' he said. 'Fine, let's do this.'

63

Holly couldn't remember a time when her heart had ever beaten so fast. The blood was roaring behind her ears, and she was struggling to steady her breath, but she refused to let Giles see that. Instead, she looked at him square on.

'You know, right? You know that Sienna's a liar? That she's a manipulator?'

'So she's not perfect. None of us are, Holly. None of us can possibly live up to your perfect expectations.'

'What's that supposed to mean?'

'Exactly what I said. You think everyone needs to be flawless. That everyone needs to be like you, or Fin, or goddam Evan.'

'Don't you *dare* bring Evan into this.' Holly's hands trembled. 'Don't you dare.'

'I have to. Don't you see that? He's there. He's always there. He'll always be there in your life, for you to compare every single person to for as long as you live. I can't compete with that. Nobody can.'

The trembling had spread past her hands now and was afflicting almost every part of her body.

'So you're just going to marry her? That's it? You know what type of person she is, and you're going to spend the rest of your life with her?'

He shrugged. 'I proposed to her.'

Holly seethed. What kind of answer was that? A bad one, and she wasn't going to let him get away with it.

'She doesn't want children, Giles. You know that. She said she'll be very persuasive, that she'll convince you it's best not to have them. That's the type of person she is, Giles. That's the type of person you are planning on marrying.'

She expected her words to elicit some sort of response. Anger, disbelief. Anything, yet there wasn't even a flicker of emotion on his face. It took only a moment to understand why.

'Faye told you,' Holly said. 'Of course she did, because she wanted you to know as much as I did. She's your sister. So you already know what Sienna's like, and you don't care? You're going to marry her anyway?'

'People change,' he said. 'Maybe she'll change.'

Holly placed her hands on her head before shaking it in disbelief. 'Really? You're going to marry a woman you know is a liar in the *hope* you can change her? Why would you do that?'

His forehead crinkled as if her question had confused him.

'Because I proposed, Holly. Because I said I wanted to spend the rest of my life with her, and I don't want to be the type of person who makes a promise like that only to break it again.'

Holly could feel the tears welling in her eyes. 'So that's it? You're going to marry her because you feel you *have* to?'

For a moment, Giles closed his eyes and pinched the bridge of his nose. 'It's what I have to do,' he said, turning to walk away, but Holly grabbed his hand.

'But my email. My first email – you read it, right?'

He scoffed. 'Yes, I read it, and I wish to hell I hadn't.'

If Holly needed any more confirmation that he didn't feel the same about her, it was becoming clearer by the second. She needed to turn around. She needed to walk away and save the tattered pieces of her heart before it was too late – but she couldn't.

'So, you don't... you don't...'

'Love you?' Giles interrupted. 'Holly, you said you *think* you love me. *Think*. Who says something like that? But you know what? It makes sense, because it's true. Of course you don't. I got engaged. I'd suddenly put another woman first in my life and *that's* when you decided to kiss me and suddenly develop feelings.'

Holly's tears turned hot with fury. 'I did *not* kiss you! You kissed me! *You* kissed *me! We only stopped because I was the one who pulled away.*'

'You think I don't know that?' His voice was a shout that trembled in her ears. 'You think I don't know that? I know that. I know I kissed you, Holly, just like I know I... I can't stop thinking about the fact that I kissed you. It's all that's going around in my head. All I want to do is kiss you again. The car journey, lunch – every minute is agony because all I want is to hold you. To pull you into me and never let go.'

Tears tumbled down Holly's cheeks.

'You said you wished you could take it back. That you would take it back in a heartbeat. That's what you said in the bar. A heartbeat.'

'The *proposal*, Holly! Not the kiss. Why the hell would I take away the most perfect thing in my life? But you only *think* you might want me. You only *think*, and that's not enough, Holly. It's not. I get it. I get that it's *you* for me. You were the person who made me a better man. You were the person I wanted to be better for. It didn't matter that I couldn't be with you, that I never thought I would be with you. I still wanted to be better for you. But you could have done this at any point, Holly. At any time, with any of the other women I dated, you could've told me you thought you might be in love with me, and I would have dropped everything like a hat for you – you know I would have. But then you did this.'

'Giles—'

He shook his head, stopping her before she could say any more.

'Do you know what the most ridiculous thing about this entire mess is? Shall I tell you? It's because of you that I'm also now the type of person I never wanted to be again. I'm a person who is engaged, who kissed somebody else, who can't stop thinking about somebody else. You wanted to talk this through, Holly, so that's what we're doing. I will lay it out all clear as day for you. Do I love Sienna the way I love you? Of course I don't. I don't think I could ever love anybody the way I love you, and I doubt you could ever love anybody the same way you loved Evan. He was the love of your life; I will never be that, just like Sienna will never be mine. Because, as ridiculous as it is, you are. You are somehow the love of my life, Holly Berry. You always have been. The moment you pushed me into that river, I was yours. Hook, line and sinker. That's how long I've loved you.'

The words took her breath away, and she moved forward, ready to respond, but Giles had his hands in the air again. Blocking her.

'The thing you need to understand, though, is I can't have my heart broken by you again. I can't have you wake up one morning and discover that you were wrong. That it was just some spur-of-the-moment jealousy thing. That you don't want to be with me. That your email was worded perfectly, and you really did just think it was love. My heart's taken two heartbreaks from you,

Holly, and that's okay. They were the right thing to do for you. I get that. But I don't think I would survive a third. So I'm going to marry Sienna. I'm going to marry Sienna because she doesn't have the power to break my heart like this, and because I made a promise.'

He drew in a long breath, and it was only then, as he wiped his cheeks, that Holly saw she wasn't the only one crying. Giles, too, had tears streaming down his face.

'We'll get back to Bourton, and then we'll work something out. A way for us to avoid seeing each other.'

'For how long?' Holly choked out, still struggling to fully comprehend everything she had just heard.

'I don't know. As long as it takes, I suppose.'

64

Giles didn't say any more. Instead, he walked out of the room, slamming the door behind him and leaving Holly standing there. She could feel the water still running from her hair down the back of her neck and the tears that continued to drip onto her chin, but she felt detached from it all. Like her body and mind had separated.

At least she had her answer now. It didn't matter if Giles loved her the way she loved him, he was engaged; he was going to be the better man and honour his relationship with Sienna, even though she didn't deserve him. A throbbing spread through her chest. How could he do that? How could he spend his life with someone like her? Someone he didn't truly love? She knew the answer, of course, as it wasn't just about the proposal. Sienna wouldn't break his heart the way that Holly had already done.

The thought caused another flurry of tears.

Why had she realised what she wanted so late? And why couldn't Giles see she would never reject him again? Never break his heart the way she had done unintentionally so many times before. If he gave her this chance, she would do everything to prove herself worthy. Why didn't he see that? Surely he knew that about her; surely he understood how much courage it had taken just to send that email admitting her feelings, but maybe it didn't matter. That was what it came down to.

She took a step towards the door. Should she go after him? Maybe that way, he would see she wasn't going to give up. Only that was what he wanted her to do, wasn't it? Forget what had ever happened between them. Move on with her life, with him no longer in it. As she turned around, she looked at the large double bed of the honeymoon suite. It would be funny if her heart wasn't broken. But it was, and how could she possibly spend the night lying in it, next to Giles, knowing what she knew now? She couldn't. For the first time since she had kissed him a fortnight ago, Holly was certain of one thing and one thing only. She needed to get out of there and as far away from Giles Caverty as possible.

Thirty minutes later, Holly was on the train, her hair roughly towel-dried, her clothes hurriedly put back on. Evelyn had been true to her word and ordered the cab for her straight away, no doubt spurred on by Holly's snivelling mess. There had been no sign of Giles.

The entire taxi journey there, she had stared at photos on her phone. How had she never noticed how many of them contained Giles before? And in how many of them were they next to each other, with their arms wrapped around one another? There had to be at least a dozen with him kissing the top of her head or with his arms wrapped fully around her. Some of them – particularly large group ones – they weren't even looking at the cameras; they were just laughing together, as if they were the only two people who mattered. She needed to delete them all. She had to, but she didn't have the strength to do that.

By her second connection of the night, Holly had realised

that her rash decision to leave without checking train timetables wasn't her smartest. She would get in after midnight and even then there wasn't a train all the way to Moreton. The Cheltenham to Bourton train ran regularly enough, or she could just get a taxi, but she didn't want to head home just yet. She needed something more. And so, as she boarded the train, she picked up her phone and dialled one of the most familiar numbers.

'Hey, how's it going? I take it it's absolute luxury? I was expecting you guys back around now; how long? How far away are you?'

Something about Jamie's voice caused the tears to thicken in Holly's throat, and she tried to swallow them back. 'Can you, can you come and pick me up from the station? From Cheltenham station,' she said.

'Holly, what is it? What's wrong? Did something happen? Please, of course, of course I can. I'm leaving now.'

'Thank you,' Holly said.

65

As Holly's train drew into the platform, she tried to work out what she was going to say to Jamie. Where the hell did she start? It was all such a mess. Though as the doors opened and Holly saw her friend standing there, the tears started again.

'What happened?' Jamie said, as Holly collapsed into her shoulder. 'Holly, what's wrong?'

Holly wanted to answer. She wanted to tell Jamie everything, only she couldn't breathe because she was sobbing so much. Her throat was raw, her lungs ached. But it was her chest that hurt the most – her heart, which felt as if it had been ripped in two.

'I messed it up. It's all so messed up,' she said.

'What is? What happened?'

'Giles and I kissed,' she said finally, meeting Jamie's gaze.

'Oh.'

Holly waited for more. For Jamie to cover her mouth in shock, or question her, prying out every detail. But that was all she said.

'Oh? That's all you've got.' Holly stepped back and raised her hands in disbelief. 'Everything is wrecked, Jamie. Everything. He doesn't want me at his wedding. He doesn't even want me in his life any more.'

Still, Jamie remained incredibly matter-of-fact about it all. 'When did this all happen? Today?'

Holly shook her head. 'No, it was after we'd been to the spa.'

For the first time, Jamie's expression showed a hint of surprise. 'The spa? But that was over two weeks ago. You didn't mention anything.'

'How could I? It's horrific. He hates me, he absolutely despises me, and I... I—'

'You love him,' she said.

'Yes. Yes. I do. I don't just think I love him. I *love* him. I love him so much, it hurts, and I know he feels the same way. He told me, but he said... he said...'

It was too late. Once again, the tears had taken over. There was no point even trying to speak. With her arms wide, Jamie brought her back in for a hug and began rubbing. The motion only seemed to accelerate the tears, although Holly couldn't tell her as much.

'It's okay. You'll be fine, I promise. We've all been wondering when it was going to hit for real. Fin and I suspected this might be why you rang. You'll be fine. We're here for you.'

'What do you mean?' Holly said. The tears momentarily halted as she looked at her friend in confusion. 'What do you mean, you've all been wondering? Who? Wondering what?'

Jamie bit down on her bottom lip sheepishly, like she'd said too much.

'Holly, this last year... Well, to be honest, I don't know how you didn't see it before. We all did. I suspect the entire village knows that you and Giles are in love. We just hoped that you'd notice before Giles did something crazy like—'

'Get engaged to someone?' Holly finished, a fresh wave of tears commencing. 'Great, So everybody's been talking about it?'

'We just care about you. That's all. Let's go home. I feel like this is a conversation we need a drink for. Come on, let's get in the car. We can talk on the way.'

Holly used the journey to fill Jamie in on everything, including the argument with Sienna, and how Giles had turned up to have a go at her, only for them to end up kissing.

'I honestly don't know if it was me or him, but I swear I was the one to break away. I was.'

'You don't need to convince me of anything here, Holly. I'm your friend.'

'But you're Giles's friend too, and I've made such a mess of things. I don't know how I fix this. What do I do?'

This was the other reason she had called Jamie to pick her up. It wasn't just about having a shoulder to cry on. Holly needed her friend to tell her what to do. How to put things right. Jamie was the most practical person she knew and right then, Holly needed her to put her practicality into sorting her life out.

'I don't know,' Jamie said. 'What do you want to do?'

Holly drew in a long breath. She knew exactly what the answer was; it was there, trembling in her lungs, but to say it out loud, that was something altogether terrifying. But then, if she couldn't say it to Jamie, how the hell was she going to say it to Giles?

'It's not because he's with someone else,' Holly said. 'I want to be with him. I want to be with him forever.'

'Then you need to tell him that.'

'I tried,' Holly said. 'He didn't want to hear it.'

'Then you need to try again. You need to make him listen.'

66

In the end, Holly decided to go for the good old-fashioned letter approach. It took her several days to decide on this, but she was certain it was the right way forward, for several reasons. First, it could be done quietly in her own home, in the evenings, when Hope was asleep. She gave herself until the end of that week, by which time, she wanted to have something truthful, heartfelt, and ready to give to Giles. It was also the approach that seemed to work in various romcoms and novels that she read, so she took that as evidence that it would be the most effective way to convey her thoughts.

On Thursday evening, Holly looked at the piece of paper in front of her and finally put her pen down for the last time. This was it, she thought, looking at her words. This was as truthful as she could get. As honest and raw. She had laid her heart out on the line, and hopefully, Giles would see it. She had said it all: how there had always been a part of her that loved him. After all, that was why she hadn't been able to stay with Ben after Hope's birth; that was why she had needed to drive a moped by herself in a strange country to speak to him on his boat before she agreed to a relationship with Evan. And yes, she knew her timing was horrific. She knew it was probably the engagement and the realisation that he would be gone forever that had given her a kick in the backside to act and do something about it. But she also knew that this wasn't some fad, that she wasn't feeling this way simply because she didn't want someone else to have him. She knew it to the very depth of her bones that if he would give her this chance, then she wouldn't let him down.

But with the letter written, there then came the issue of delivery.

'I can't give it to him directly,' Holly said to Jamie that evening as she handed her the envelope. 'He won't speak to me. He'll probably just burn it up there and then. I need you to do it. And I need you to do it at a time when Sienna won't be there.'

'Really? They're practically living together now.'

'I know, but you can make it happen, right? Why don't you ask him round to babysit the twins?'

Jamie's eyebrow rose. 'He wouldn't buy that,' Jamie said. 'Why would I ask him when I have you next door?'

'Okay, then maybe Fin could invite him for a round of golf or something, and you could see him and give it to him then. But you have to make sure he reads it, okay? You can't let him just put it in his pocket.'

Jamie let out a sigh. 'You're not making this easy, you know. Just talk to him.'

The way Jamie said it made it sound so simple. Like it was an option Holly hadn't thought of.

'He won't pick up when I call him. I have tried. I really have. He won't even reply to messages. I've sent him one almost every day since we got back and he hasn't replied to any of them.'

'Perhaps he hasn't seen them,' Jamie suggested.

It was Holly's turn to raise an eyebrow. 'Please, the letter is the only way. I really need you to give it to him.'

Jamie tightened her lips ever so slightly. 'Okay, leave it with me. I'll think of something.'

'Before the weekend,' Holly said. 'I'm not sure I can last any longer than that.'

'Okay, I will try, but I'm not making any promises. It's only because I think that you two are destined to be together that I'm doing this. You know that.'

'You do?' The comment caught Holly by surprise. They had talked about the situation at length, but it mainly involved Holly crying about having messed things up so royally, and not letting Jamie get a word in edgeways. And while Jamie had made it apparent that she thought something like this *would* happen countless times, she'd never implied that she thought it *should* happen.

'Of course I do,' Jamie replied. 'I mean, you bring out the best in each other, don't you?'

'I'm not sure he brings out the best in me,' Holly said. 'He makes me furious and hot-headed.'

'And sometimes, you need a bit of that,' Jamie said. 'Sometimes, you need someone who allows you to get angry about stuff. Anyway, I'll work out a way to get this to him.' She gestured to the envelope.

'And you'll let me know as soon as he's read it?'

'Yes,' Jamie said. 'But only if you stop nagging me about it. Otherwise, Giles might not be the one to burn it. I'll do it myself.'

67

If Holly had thought that writing the letter was difficult, waiting for it to be delivered and read was even worse. She was working at the sweet shop every day, which was good in the sense that it kept her distracted and busy, but bad in that her inability to focus meant she kept making mistakes.

'I asked for marzipan teacakes, not coconut teacakes,' one customer said.

Another grumbled, 'Liquorice bullets? I asked for Liquorice Allsorts. I can't stand liquorice bullets – they're too hard on my teeth. I thought you knew that.'

'Sorry, sorry,' Holly said, putting the wrong sweets back and collecting the correct jar from the shelves. 'Yes, of course. My mistake. Let me sort that out now.'

'Are you sure you're okay?' her father asked on Friday when he popped into the shop. 'You don't seem quite yourself. Do you think you're coming down with something? You know your mother's had a terrible head cold these last few weeks. Perhaps you've caught it from her.'

'You're right,' Holly lied. 'Perhaps I have.'

Unfortunately, her confession to an imaginary illness didn't get her father off her case quite as easily as she'd hoped.

'Well, you don't want to pass it on to any customers,' he continued. 'Perhaps you shouldn't be in.'

'It'll be fine,' Holly said. 'I'm fine.'

'I'd ring Greta if I were you. Or I can cover if you'd like.'

'Honestly, Dad. I'll be fine. I'm sure I'll be feeling right as rain tomorrow.'

'Well, if you're not, I'd book an appointment at the doctor's. The last thing you want is to be out of action when the summer season hits in full.'

'Okay. Yes, Dad. I will.'

Holly would have breathed a sigh of relief when her dad finally left, only while he had been happy to believe her excuse about a head cold, Caroline was not.

'Something is going on with you,' she said. 'I know it is, and I know whatever it is Jamie knows too because I asked her, and she was all funny with me, and that doesn't normally happen. I don't understand. Are you dating somebody? Is that what it is?'

Holly let out a long groan. She loved Caroline to bits, and she also knew that there was no way her friend was going to drop the issue. So rather than sticking with her original excuse or even manufacturing another, it just seemed easier to relent.

'If I tell you, that is it. I tell you and then we let it go. It is not up for discussion. I don't want to talk about it. I don't even want to tell you, but you probably deserve to know, so I'm going to. After that though, I don't want to talk about it or anything to do with it. I don't want to hear the names of the people I mention to you heard under this roof. Or at all. Ever. Understood?'

'Understood,' Caroline said, using her finger to mark a cross over her heart, the way they used to do when they were at school. 'So I was right. There is something going on?'

'There is.'

The corners of Caroline's mouth twitched excitedly. 'Is it to do with Giles? Is it to do with him getting married? Have you suddenly realised that you're in love with him and don't want him to be with anyone else?'

'Why do you say that?'

'Oh my God!' Caroline squealed. 'That's amazing. Michael and I were taking bets on when you'd realise. So have you told Giles already?'

Holly let out a groan. 'Did everybody see I was in love with Giles except me?'

'Maybe Giles too. I think he just didn't want to admit it to himself. You know, in case he got his hopes up and you broke his heart. Again.'

Holly stifled a bitter laugh. The fact that anyone could think she would be the one to break Giles's heart when she was the one completely broken could have been amusing, if it didn't hurt so damn much.

'So, are you going to tell him?' Caroline said, a grin spreading on her face as she clapped her hands excitedly. 'Oh my God, this is amazing! I mean, it's terrible for Sienna, but really, I've had stomach bugs that have been around longer than she has and honestly, I think she's a bit of a bitch. So when are you going to do it? When are you going to tell him you're in love with him? What are you going to say?'

Holly rolled her eyes. 'Do you remember me saying I didn't want to discuss this at all? This feels like a discussion.'

'I just need a couple more details.' Caroline's eyes begged her. 'I just want to know when you're going to tell him.'

Holly let out a long sigh. This was why she didn't want to talk about it. Because it meant reliving the humiliation again.

'I did. I already told him.'

'You did?' Caroline's hand flew up to her mouth. 'This is amazing!'

'No, I'm afraid it's not. It's not going to happen.'

Caroline's jaw hung open. 'What? You can't be serious. He adores you.'

'Well, apparently, that's not enough, and it's okay. Maybe... I mean, he doesn't trust that I won't break his heart, and I get that, so I've written him a letter, and Jamie is going to deliver it, and we'll just have to see what he says.'

'Oh my God, this is... this is bizarre,' Caroline said. 'You and Giles Caverty. At freaking last!'

Holly couldn't help but laugh. 'It is not a given thing. Giles is engaged, remember? And he's all about doing the right thing now. That includes not breaking off engagements.'

'Right, right. But let's be honest, none of us really liked her, did we?'

'You're not helping, Caroline.'

'I thought I was.'

Holly shook her head, though she had to admit that talking to Caroline about it had made her feel better. There was a lightness about it, a good humour. Whenever she spoke to Jamie about the situation, she always ended up in tears; this was good.

'This is actually completely amazing news,' Caroline continued. 'Think of it this way: even if it doesn't work out between you two, it's a sign that you can love again, right? I think for a long time, you thought that wasn't possible. Now you know it is. You're ready to put yourself out there and find someone who adores you. That's got to be a win.'

'Maybe,' Holly said. It was definitely a good way to look at things, but she wasn't convinced she'd ever be able to put her heart on the line again after this. This was it. She could feel it in her very bones. It was Giles or no one. And she was about to say as much when she glanced out the window and saw Jamie walking towards her. Her expression was serious. Her hands clenched at her sides.

Holly's heart did a double somersault and landed somewhere near the top of her throat. She knew without a doubt what that meant. Jamie had done it; she had given Giles the letter.

'Hey, Caroline,' Jamie said as she walked into the shop. 'I just need to grab Holly for a minute.'

Within an instant, Caroline had sprung around from the counter, shut the front door, and switched the sign to *Closed*.

'Like hell you do! I'm still on the first part; I need to know about this. Whatever's going on, I'm 100 per cent in.'

Jamie looked at Holly.

'So you finally told her about the kiss?'

'What?' Caroline said. 'She didn't say there was a kiss. You kissed him? You told me you were in love with him.'

This was not what Holly wanted. She wanted to find out what Giles had said to Jamie, but Caroline was involved now too. She might as well know everything.

'Well, I only realised I loved him after I kissed him. I told him up in Anglesey and he said he wouldn't risk a relationship with me, so I wrote him a letter to tell him there was no risk. I was all his. That's pretty much it.' At this, she turned to her other friend. 'Did you give it to him? Did you give him the letter?'

Jamie nodded. That was it, a single nod. Could she not tell Holly needed more? Her heart was racing, adrenaline coursing through her veins and there was a very good chance she was going to be sick.

'And... did he read it? Could you watch him read it?'

'I did.'

'And how did he look? What did he say?'

'I don't know. He... he got a pen, and he wrote on it and he asked me to give it back to you.'

'What?' Holly said.

Jamie reached into her bag and pulled out the letter. 'I don't know what it says. I didn't read it. And he wasn't writing for very long. Are you sure you want to do this here? Maybe I should've waited till you got home.'

'No, no, this is what I wanted. I wanted to know as soon as possible.'

Jamie still held the letter in her hand. The seal was broken, and the paper inside was slightly crumpled. He had, without a doubt, taken it out and read it. He knew exactly how Holly felt.

'He wrote something on it?'

'I think so,' Jamie said.

Holly nodded. 'I think I might go upstairs, if you don't mind,' she said, taking the envelope from Jamie.

'Of course not.'

'Go.'

When Holly's foot was on the bottom step of the staircase, she hesitated. 'Actually, no. I've changed my mind. I think I'd like you guys here.' She drew in a long breath, which she blew back out as she tried to steady her pulse. 'Okay, here goes. Wish me luck.'

68

Holly pulled the crumbled piece of paper out of the envelope. She had taken up the entirety of the front side of the A4, and several lines on the back page too, but it still left almost three-quarters of a side for Giles's message. Plenty of room for him to scribble down a thorough, heartfelt response. That was what she thought, at least, until she turned the paper over and saw the words he had written.

'He's an arse,' Caroline said. 'He is. I always said he'd go back to his old ways. People like him can't change. Not deep down. He's rotten to the core.'

'He's not rotten to the core,' Holly said. 'And he's not gone back to his old ways. He's just protecting himself, that's all.'

'Still, it's pretty harsh,' Jamie said.

But it's true, Holly thought as she stared at the sentence written on the page in front of her.

Sometimes love isn't enough.

That was it. That was his final say. Love wasn't enough.

Funny how all the songs and movies said that it was. That love could conquer everything. For so long, Holly had believed that. She'd believed that if or when she found true love again, it would be the final piece she needed to make life perfect. But now she knew the truth. It wasn't enough.

They shut up the shop and headed upstairs, although Holly wasn't sure why. She felt perfectly capable of working; she felt strangely okay. Numb, that's how people would probably describe it. Numb. But that wasn't a bad thing, was it? It was definitely better than feeling the pain she knew would come if she let it in.

'Honestly,' she said, 'it's okay. I think it's for the best.'

'You're joking, right?' Caroline said. 'This is insane. He's not going to be happy. We can all see that. The only reason he proposed to her is because he had an accident and some sudden crisis of faith, like he thought if he didn't get married immediately and have children, his whole life was going to end. That's the truth of it.'

Holly wasn't going to defend Giles there. Not when she knew it was the truth.

'It doesn't matter why he proposed to her; he did it, and he's going to see it through. I respect him for that.'

'You respect him for marrying a woman who's not the one he loves?'

'Would you just drop it?' Holly didn't mean to snap. She didn't, but she couldn't hear this any more. 'I'm sorry, I'm sorry. I just... I need some space, okay? Can you open up the shop again? There are still a couple of hours of trading left.'

She stood up and took her bag from the table.

'Where are you going?' Jamie said. 'What are you going to do?'

'I'm going to pick up Hope,' Holly replied. 'I'm going to remember how amazing my world is, because she's in it, and then I'm going to move on with my life. It would be great if you guys would let me do that.'

69

Holly walked towards the school, only to realise it was twenty minutes before the children would be let out, leaving her with nothing to do other than stand alone with her thoughts. But that was good, wasn't it? In fact, if she looked at it objectively, the whole situation was positive. She'd had her heart broken. So what? It wasn't the first time it had happened. If Dan hadn't broken her heart by cheating on her, she would never have ended up in Bourton with the sweet shop and with Hope. And having a broken heart was a lot easier than what she went through with Evan. She would pick herself up and come out of this situation stronger. Yes, it would probably take a long time for her and Giles to rebuild their friendship, but in all fairness, nobody ever thought they would do that after the whole 'sabotaging the sweet shop' fiasco. Just like nobody thought that she and Ben would be able to co-parent Hope so well. It would require some adjusting; that was all.

What she needed to do was find a big enough distraction that would let her move on with her life and push Giles Caverty as far out of her system as possible. A new project, something to do with work, perhaps. And that was the moment she remembered.

With a burst of energy, she turned away from the school gates. Twenty minutes. That was definitely long enough to run home and back, provided she actually ran and, while it wasn't common for Holly to be seen sprinting down the high street, she could reach a fair pace if needed. And at that moment, she needed to run.

It didn't matter that her question could be asked just as easily in half an hour, an hour, or even a day's time. It didn't matter that Fin would be coming to pick his three up from school and if she hung on for fifteen minutes, she would see him anyway. She needed to talk to him. Now.

When she reached the house, she didn't take out her key. Instead, panting from the exertion of the run, she knocked repeatedly on Fin and Jamie's door.

'Hey, Holly. Are you okay? Jamie's going to be back in fifteen. Do you want to wait in here? I can pick up Hope if that helps.'

There was something about his expression and the way he was speaking to her, as if she might, at any second, crumble into a heap, that told Holly Jamie had spoken to him about the Giles situation. But she wasn't here to talk about Giles. Not at all.

'I'm good. Great, actually. That friend of yours, the one who's starting the old-fashioned sweet shops in the States. I don't suppose I could have his number today?'

70

Holly couldn't believe how quickly everything had moved, though most of that was due to her taking a month to make contact. In business terms, a lot could happen in that length of time. But on the same day as she received Giles's response, she had also finally spoken on the phone to Moritz, Fin's friend in America, and now, five days later, she was packing her bags.

'I wish I could come with you. I want to come with you,' Hope said. 'We could see Aunty Erin. See Nanny and Grandad.'

'I know, I know we could, but if this works out, then maybe we'll get to spend quite a bit of time in America. How would you like that? Besides, Rhubarb needs a lot of fuss. You know she gets funny when I go away.'

Holly thought that mentioning the kitten would provide an adequate distraction, but she should have known better.

'What does "quite a bit" mean?' Hope asked. 'I wouldn't be leaving Daddy and Georgia?'

'No, no, of course not, but maybe we could go for a couple of months in the summer. How does that sound? And Christmas too. I don't think you remember Christmas in America properly, but the snow was amazing.'

'I thought it was hot at Christmas in America?'

'Depends on which part you go to. We could go to a hot part one year and a cold part another year. How does that sound?'

'Could we bring Rhubarb?' Hope asked. Holly rolled her eyes. *Now she remembers the kitten.*

On the drive to the airport, Jamie didn't hold anything back. 'This is running away – you know that. That's all you're doing.'

'I don't know what you're on about,' Holly replied. 'I'm not running away; I'm thinking of myself and my career. Moritz has offered me an amazing consulting fee, and all I have to do is fly to the States every couple of months to check how the new branches are opening up. It sounds perfect.'

'It sounds like an excuse to ignore your feelings,' she said. 'Which we all know you're very good at.'

Holly shot her a sharp look. 'What do you want me to do?' she said, looking at her. 'I told him. I told him how I feel. He doesn't feel the same.'

'That's not true, and you know it's not.'

'Okay, well, he's not willing to take that risk, and I understand that.' Holly just wanted to drop the subject, but Jamie was hanging on tooth and nail.

'You should fight for him,' she said.

'I did, three times. I sent an email, I told him in person, and I wrote a letter. I'm not doing any more than that, Jamie. That's not how this works. I know people say you should fight for the one you love, but maybe if they're the ones for you, you shouldn't be put in a position where you have to.' She paused. 'Who knows? Maybe I'll find another dashing American.'

Jamie smiled, fleetingly. 'As long as you're sure.'

'I am. Thank you.'

Half an hour later, Jamie pulled into a car parking space and cut the engine. 'Are you sure you don't want me to come in with you? You're really early, you know. I don't mind hanging around for a bit.'

'It's fine,' Holly said. 'I've got a good book. I'll just read.'

'Stay in touch, right? When you board, when you land. When you get to Moritz's?'

'It's three days, Jamie, that's all. I'm gone for three days.'

Jamie shrugged as she grinned. 'What can I say? I like having a neighbour.'

71

Holly had only been planning on taking hand luggage, but then Moritz had asked her to bring samples of sweets so that they could do taste comparisons to ones he could get Stateside. So instead, she was lugging a massive suitcase towards the check-in desk. None of which were open, despite the sizeable queue that had already formed.

This trip wasn't only about sweet tasting, though they were hoping to narrow down suppliers. They were also looking at interior design, uniform and general product branding, so they were ready with a hard launch across country. It was a far cry from just hoping to get through the day and selling enough sugar mice to be approved for a mortgage, the way Holly had done when she started her business, but the fact that Moritz was paying for all expenses, along with a consultancy fee, was a sure sign of how much he valued her knowledge.

She was also hopefully going to fit in a meet-up with Catherine, one of Evan's sisters, while she was there too, as long as she could get the day off work.

Talking of dates, she couldn't help but wonder if Giles and

Sienna had settled on one yet. It had been less than a week since he had unequivocally put to rest any idea of him and Holly in a relationship. Since then, she'd heard nothing from, or about, him. Jamie, Caroline and Ben had obviously decided amongst themselves that Giles's name was not to be raised in front of her, and the only person who had mentioned him at all was Hope asking when he was next coming around. Holly had brushed off the comment, saying he was busy with work, then helped Holly set up a cat-training rink for Rhubarb to keep her occupied. Thankfully, it worked, although any chance of Rhubarb appearing on the silver screen in the near future felt unlikely.

As Holly stood in the queue, she fired off another quick message to Jamie. Thanking her for the lift, and also for looking after Rhubarb. Again. Then she made a video for Ben to show Hope when she got home from school, given that Holly would be in the air by then and unable to speak to her until the morning.

Holly groaned. The queue didn't appear to be moving at all. She had hoped to do a bit of duty-free browsing on the other side of departures, but it was looking less and less likely.

Finally, two air stewardess appeared. Although rather than heading behind the counter and taking people's luggage, as Holly had expected, the pair moved into the centre of the queue, where the woman cleared her throat several times, trying to get every-one's attention.

'Ladies and gentlemen, this is an announcement for those who are booked on the Miami flight.'

Holly's ears pricked as her stomach churned. She really didn't want the flight to be cancelled. It would mean another day of rejigging the sweet-shop rotas, not to mention getting in late for Moritz. It would be a hassle she didn't want to deal with, yet she knew there was no positive reason for an air hostess to be addressing them in this manner.

'Ladies and gentlemen, we want to inform you that this flight has been overbooked.'

'Overbooked?' a man in front of Holly said. 'What's that meant to mean? Surely you know how many seats are on the plane?'

Similar rumbles rattled throughout the queue.

Before Evan, Holly had never realised that airlines frequently overbooked their flights, on the assumption that a couple of people wouldn't come, and they would make a few extra quid. She also knew that if you volunteered to get bumped onto the next flight, they would normally give you a nice chunk of money for it, and had it been another time in her life, she would've probably jumped at that option. But right now, it just wasn't feasible. She wanted to get on that plane, to see Moritz and to feel like she was doing something productive. So, when the air stewardess asked if any passengers would mind moving to the next day's flight, Holly stayed silent. As, it appeared, did everybody else.

'Unfortunately, if we do not get some volunteers, some people will have no choice but to be reassigned to a later flight,' she said. 'If you do change your mind, please let myself or another member of staff know.'

From the volume of grumbling, Holly didn't think the air stewardess was going to get her wish as she and her partner slipped behind the counter and finally began taking people's baggage.

A flutter of nerves filled Holly's stomach. There was another reason she didn't want to change flights, though it was hard to admit, even to herself. This was going to be the longest flight she had ever done on her own, and now that she was here, she couldn't help but worry. The last thing she needed was to be bumped from this flight and have to start the worry all over again. But she wouldn't have to change, would she? After all, she was just over halfway back in the queue, and they weren't going to bump half the people, were they?

With the check-in desks now open, the queue crawled forward, inch by inch. Finally, she reached the front.

'Going to Miami?' the woman said as Holly placed her passport on the desk.

'Yes,' Holly replied. 'Yes, I—'

'No, no, she's not.'

The voice was enough to cause her heart to jolt. She was wrong, wasn't she? She was hearing things. As her throat tightened, Holly's eyes filled with tears. She didn't want to look around and see she was wrong. But she couldn't just stand there. And so, with her hand trembling, Holly shifted her gaze.

'You were seriously just going to leave?' he said.

'Excuse me?' Holly didn't know how she was meant to react. Giles was there. He was there, looking at her for the first time since she'd properly confessed her love. And he looked mad. But before she could speak, he snatched up her passport from the counter. 'What are you doing?'

'You're going to take a job in America?'

'It's not—'

'Of all the irresponsible things you could do. I mean, it's one thing only thinking about yourself now, but what about Hope?'

'Excuse me?'

Giles shook his head, as if he couldn't believe Holly was actually going away for three days. Like people didn't do that? Like Hope didn't have Ben there to look after her.

'Caroline told me; she told me everything. She told me that you're going to take this job, and you're going to move to the other side of the world, to be closer to Evan's family.'

'She did?'

'And that once you've got everything sorted, Ben's going to

send Hope over for six months a year. Six months! Why would you do that, Holly? How? How could you do that?'

'Caroline told you this?' Holly pinched the bridge of her nose. Caroline knew exactly what the situation was with Holly's job. She was the one covering the extra shifts at the shop. So why would she tell Giles such a ridiculous lie? And how the hell could he believe she would do that to Hope? She opened her mouth to say as much, but Giles was still going.

'You're doing this to punish me, right? That's what this is about. So not only do I have to lose you, but Hope too. You know how much I love her. And she adores me too. You know that. Of all the things—'

'Giles, Caroline has—'

'Excuse me, ma'am, could you please move to the side or give your passport back? We have quite a queue behind you.'

Holly tried to pull her passport out of Giles's hand.

'Sorry,' she said, 'yes. Just give me a moment.' But he was holding on too tightly. If she pulled any harder, she was going to rip it in two, and then she definitely wouldn't be getting on the flight.

'No, you don't get to do this,' Giles said. 'You don't just get to pack up and leave because things have got difficult and not gone the way you want. It's cowardly, Holly.'

That was it. Holly had heard enough.

'For God's sake, will you listen to me? Caroline engineered this. I am not moving to America.'

Giles's eyes widened. 'But you're here? And you've got a massive suitcase.'

'Which is filled with sweets. Yes, I am going for a job, but I'm not moving. It's just a couple of days every few months, that's all.'

'It is? Then why did Caroline think—?' It finally sank in. 'She knew. She knew what I was going to do. She knew that I couldn't...'

'Ma'am, I really need you to move to the side. Otherwise, I will have to get you removed. Both of you.'

'Fine. But I am getting on this flight. You're not bumping me because of this.'

Grabbing her bag, Holly shifted to the side. She knew people were staring at her. Watching them, but she couldn't move any further. Her legs wouldn't let her. It had been less than two weeks since she had seen Giles. Half a month. Having him there, within touching distance, caused an ache to spread through her chest. It didn't help how much he had changed, either. His face was dark with stubble – which was a long way from his normal, clean-shaven look. No doubt it was a request, or rather a demand, from Sienna.

'You can go back home now, Giles,' Holly said, her teeth gritted in anger. 'I'm not abandoning my daughter, and as for the cowardly comment, I think you need to take a good hard look in the mirror there.'

His hand hung by his side. Holly used the moment to grab the passport. This time, it slipped out of his grip with ease. 'Go back to Sienna, Giles. You have a wedding to plan. And I have a future to build.'

She was partway through turning around when he spoke again.

'The wedding's off.'

'What?' There it was again. The jolt in her heart. Like it had suddenly forgotten how to beat properly.

'We got into a big argument, and she ended things.'

'An argument?' Holly said. 'About what?' She had a horrible feeling she already knew the answer.

'About children in the wedding. She wanted to have all the little kids as flower girls and page boys, then not invite them to the reception, or something. It all escalated, and she walked out.'

Holly nodded. That sounded like an incredibly Sienna thing to want.

'I'm sure you can fix things if you want to.'

He nodded. 'I'm sure you're right. But it was a while ago now. When we got back from Anglesey.'

'What?' That was almost two weeks ago. Why hadn't he said something?

'I think I was spoiling for a fight, if I'm honest,' Giles continued. 'You know, giving her a reason to break up with me.'

Silence followed.

'So it's over?' Holly said, not sure why she couldn't stop swallowing.

'It is,' Giles said.

A flicker of hope formed in Holly's heart, but she quashed it before it could catch light.

'But it doesn't change anything, does it? You told me yourself, love isn't always enough.' A new throbbing began behind her ribs, while the heat of tears burned behind her eyes. 'When I wrote you that letter, you weren't even with her, but you still didn't want me.'

'Of course I want you! I want to be with you more than anything.'

'But you—'

He stepped towards her.

'I messed up, Holly. I wanted to put things right between us, but I needed to do right by Sienna too. After everything I did to her, she was owed a bit of respect. Believe me, the minute it was over, I wanted to drive straight over to you, but that wouldn't have been right. Not after calling off the engagement. That's why I stayed away. Because I knew I'd have no restraint if I saw you. Besides, I'd been horrible to you in Anglesey. I was trying to work out how to apologise. But then I got your letter and it was perfect. So perfect. I just felt... inadequate. Like I'd never be deserving of your love. So I thought it would be better if I pushed you away. That maybe, if I believed you hated me, I could stop loving you quite so much. But it didn't work. Not at all.'

'Giles, I—'

'Oh screw this,' he said.

Without another word, he swept her into his arms. It was a kiss that belonged in the movies. In a happily ever after. A kiss that told Holly everything had suddenly fallen into place and nothing would ever be in doubt again. As he pulled her closer, she felt the fear fly out of him too. This was how it was meant to be. This was always how it was meant to be.

A chorus of cheers went up behind them, and when they broke apart, a hearty blush coloured Holly's cheeks. Giles, on the other hand, wore a grin that stretched from ear to ear. Still holding her hand, he lifted it up to his lips as if she was going to place a kiss there, only to hesitate.

'You took your ring off,' he said.

'I did. Before Anglesey.'

'Why? That ring's a part of you, Holly. Evan's part of you. And I wouldn't change anything about that.'

'I love you so much,' she said.

'The feeling's mutual.'

She moved towards him. Her pulse drumming as she knew another kiss was only a heartbeat away, but before their lips touched, a loud throat-clearing stopped them.

Holly turned to find the air stewardess, and everyone else, looking at them.

'Excuse me, ma'am, do I take this to mean you aren't getting the flight?'

Holly looked up to Giles, where a glint in his eyes said it all.

'You know what?' she said to the air hostess. 'I think I'll take that flight bump after all.'

EPILOGUE

Holly Berry had always heard the phrase, 'You should fall in love with your best friend,' but she had never thought that would happen to her. Yet, somehow, it had. She was in love with her best friend, Giles Caverty, and nothing had ever felt more natural or more like home.

She had thought there would be a transition period – that it might take Hope some time to get used to the idea of Giles being more than just a close family friend. It didn't.

'You know it was obvious, right?' she'd said. 'I could always tell you had crushes on each other.'

'What do you know about crushes?!' Holly had replied. 'You're way too young for those?'

'Am I? Weird.'

Holly chose not to respond to that one. She was just grateful Hope was happy. Three months after that airport incident, he moved into hers. Everything slotted together perfectly. She went over to the States every three months to offer Moritz advice on his ever-expanding sweet shop empire over there and Giles's support offered her all the confidence she needed to set up a second Just One More up the road in Lower Slaughter.

A year later, on a Wednesday afternoon, they headed out for a drive in Giles's car. It was still one of their favourite things to do, and they promised Hope that when summer came around, they would get a campervan so they could go on proper driving adventures. That day, however, it was just the two of them as Giles pulled up beside a small footpath and turned to face her.

'Why are you stopping?' she said. 'Is everything okay?'

'Yeah, everything's fine. Only I've been thinking about something a lot lately,' he said.

'Really? That's not like you,' Holly teased.

Giles shook his head and laughed. 'I've been thinking about the right way to ask you something. And it's been stressing me out. But then, when we came out today, it struck me. There is no right way, because there is no wrong way. And if there is no wrong way, then that means there can't be a right way either. You understand?'

'I'm not sure,' Holly replied. 'Actually, Giles, it sounds a little bit like you're babbling there. You know what I think about babbling.'

He chuckled.

'Well, let me ask another way then,' he said. 'One that doesn't require any talking at all.' He reached into his pocket and pulled out a small, round box. 'Holly Berry,' he said, 'will you marry me?'

She didn't need to think about the answer. She didn't even reply with words.

Instead, her lips landed straight on his. It wasn't the type of proposal some people would have wanted. He hadn't gotten down on one knee and the ring box was still closed, so Holly had no idea what the ring looked like, but it didn't matter. There could have been a piece of string inside and she would have said yes.

A feeling of pure happiness flooded her, only for a sudden thought to make her jolt back.

'What is it?' he asked, concerned.

'Well, I can't take your surname,' she said.

'Why not? Don't you like Caverty?'

'You can't have a sweet shop owner with the surname Cavity!' she exclaimed.

Giles's head tilted to the side.

'Wow, cavities and sweets. I've never noticed that before.'

* * *

MORE FROM HANNAH LYNN

Another book from Hannah Lynn, *The Side Hustle*, is available to order now here:

https://mybook.to/SideHustleBackAd

ACKNOWLEDGEMENTS

I can't believe this is the end! Of all the books I have written, the connection between myself and the sweet shop is so very personal, and I adored writing every book in this series (even though book seven was a weepy one. Sorry about that!).

I am so grateful to you, my readers, who have come on this journey with me. It wouldn't have been possible to bring all these stories to life without you and I'm so appreciative of every one of you.

As always, my biggest thanks in this series goes to Nina. Twenty-six years later, and I can still remember my first day at the sweet shop, carrying boxes of fudge up the stairs and spending a morning pricing them all up. In fact, I have so many memories of my time there, and all of them are filled with joy. I remember the old gentlemen who always had his peppermint creams packed in a tin he brought from home, and the way we would spend the weeks before Christmas making endless bows to put on the gold boxes of Belgium chocolates. Most of all, I remember the looks on the customers' faces when they discovered we sold some old childhood favourite they hadn't had for years and were suddenly transported back decades. That job was not just a way for me to earn my first bit of money; it was fundamental in forming the foundations of who I was to become, and I do not have enough words to say thank you for taking a chance on me (and putting up with my mess!).

Thank you to my editor Emily and the team who work so hard to ensure you are getting the best version of this book.

And lastly, thank you to Jake and Elsie for their unending support and understanding. I guess I can't say I have to go and buy sweets as research any more!

ABOUT THE AUTHOR

Hannah Lynn is the author of over twenty books spanning several genres. Hannah grew up in the Cotswolds, UK. After graduating from university, she spent 15 years as a teacher of physics, teaching in the UK, Thailand, Malaysia, Austria and Jordan.

Sign up to Hannah Lynn's mailing list here for news, competitions and updates on future books.

Visit Hannah's website: www.hannahlynnauthor.com

Follow Hannah on social media:

facebook.com/hannahlynnauthor

instagram.com/hannahlynnwrites

bookbub.com/authors/hannah-lynn

Boldwood

Boldwood Books is an award-winning fiction publishing company seeking out the best stories from around the world.

Find out more at www.boldwoodbooks.com

Join our reader community for brilliant books, competitions and offers!

Follow us
@BoldwoodBooks
@TheBoldBookClub

Sign up to our weekly deals newsletter

https://bit.ly/BoldwoodBNewsletter